The Percentages Men

A Novel by
Brendan Gisby

ISBN: 1491237627
ISBN-13: 978-1491237625

All characters are fictional, and any resemblance to anyone living or dead is accidental.

A McStorytellers publication

http://www.mcstorytellers.com

Contents

Prologue

Morocco, 2003

When he opened his eyes again and saw that the desert sky had turned purple, Jimbo knew for certain he would die soon. There would be no last-minute rescue; no miracle. Spread-eagled, unable to move, his blood seeping into the sand beneath him, his life ebbing away, he knew he would take his last breath out there, alone in that vastness, a speck in the Sahara.

As the night grew blacker, stars began to appear – a few at first, then thousands more all at once, then many thousands more until the sky resembled a giant *Star Wars* screen, flickering and glistening, lighting up the desert floor, zooming down to meet him. The stars were so close now that if he had been able to raise an arm he could have reached up and touched the nearest one.

In the starlight, Jimbo could make out objects lying in the sand on either side of him. Over there on his left was his rucksack, half empty now, the rest of its contents strewn around it. His mobile phone had been in the rucksack. He could imagine it ringing some time the next day, when Sally's flight landed. It would ring again when she arrived at the villa in Marrakech. Then it would ring again and again and again in the empty desert, the intervals between the calls becoming shorter as panic set in. Sally wasn't the brightest spark in the box, so it would take her a while to raise the alarm. But by then all that would be left of him was a carcass half-eaten by the desert dogs.

Uncharacteristically, Jimbo felt a pang of sympathy for Sally, for the trauma she would go through, the pain she would suffer. *Sorry it had to end this way, Sal. So sorry, princess.*

The feeling passed quickly. He found himself peering at the two objects on his right. They were what was left of his laptop, the screen and the keyboard now separate pieces embedded in the sand, standing erect like tombstones. He had brought the laptop with him just in case. *In case of what, eh? In case I decided to send that email to Neville? That one last offer to return the money to him. That one last plea for him to grow some balls and get rid of the snake. Yeah, well it's too fucking late for that now. It wouldn't have changed anything anyway. The deal was done too long ago and it could never be undone now. I should have accepted then that I wasn't part of the company any longer. The company I poured my heart and soul into... until that cunt...*

Jimbo sighed. He couldn't see any sign of it from where he lay, but he knew his motorbike was out there somewhere. He remembered it skidding on its side across the sand and him being propelled into the air to somersault and then crash to the ground on his back. He loved that old bike. A Matchless 500, one of the few built in the Sixties. He had bought it in 1974, when he was just a teenager and barely able to handle it. He had cleaned it up and kept it running ever since. He brought it over with him from Belfast when he started his new life in Edinburgh. And only that week he had ridden it all the way from Edinburgh over to Calais, down through France and Spain and across to Morocco. The old girl hadn't let him down once. But then she had to go and hit a rock hidden in the sand and his head had to smash down on another. *Jeez, all this rippling golden sand for hundreds of miles around, and I happen to find the only two fucking boulders in the place.*

He thought it was ironic that the only thing he had ever cherished in the world should also be the cause of his downfall. But he supposed he had no-one else to blame but himself. The trip to Marrakech had been much tougher than he had anticipated. He had had to fight hard to concentrate, to keep his attention on the road, while all the time his mind was in turmoil. Those same questions pounded his brain over and over and over again. *Why did you give up, Jimbo? What got into you? What made you agree to sell your shares back to Neville? Did he give you a fair deal? Or did the slimy cunt fuck you over? You've got some money now, sonny, but it won't last for ever. What are you going to do for the rest of your life? You're lost, Jimbo. In a wilderness. And it's all that bastard Lamb's doing. Why can't Neville understand that Lamb's only out for himself, not the company? Their company...*

Anger and resentment had boiled up in him, so much so that he had to stop frequently on the way until he calmed down. Then, instead of resting when he arrived at the villa, he had showered and gone straight out again, making a beeline for the desert. He wanted the Saharan wind to blast his face and tear through his hair; he wanted the wind to clear all the shit, all the badness, out of his head. So it wasn't long before he strapped his helmet to the pillion and left the road. That vast, shimmering sea of flatness, stretching away to infinity, was so tempting. He had always dreamed of taking the old girl out into the desert, opening her up and letting her do what she was built for. It was like swimming with dolphins, he supposed, one of those things you should do before you die. *Aye, well, Jimbo, you've certainly fulfilled that dream, so you have. But you weren't meant to die into the bargain, you tube.*

He tried to smile at his own joke, at the stupidity of it all, but he couldn't move his lips. He knew he was growing stiff and cold out there in the desert at night, but he didn't feel cold or anything else; only a numbness, a drowsiness. He was sure there wasn't long to go.

He had heard that your whole life flashed before your eyes in the moments before you died. He thought perhaps that was what was happening to him, because now he had a clear picture in his mind of that little red-bricked, terraced house where he was brought up. Then the words of a song thrust themselves at him, uninvited, unwelcome: *In a neat little town they called Belfast...*

He couldn't understand why the words of *The Black Velvet Band* should come to him at this time. He had always hated that song. And he couldn't stand The Dubliners, who had sung it and made it more popular than it should ever have been. *Another bunch of Taigs with beards. Almost as bad as those Clancy cunts with their moronic jerseys and so-called rebel songs. The UVF should have shot them all.*

He wondered if he was sounding like his Da. That sour-faced bastard he used to call his father. The war hero with one leg, who never had a good word for anyone, Protestant or Catholic, and least of all for his own son, his only child. It had been a relief when the ould sod kicked the bucket.

He wondered why his Ma and Da had waited for so long before they had him. Fuck, they were old when he was born. His pals at school used to think they were his grandparents, so they did!

And he wondered about his Ma. Still alive, still living in that wee house on that quiet wee street on the edge of Belfast. She was as old as the hills now, as old as the hills that overlooked the house. How would she take the news that her Jimbo had gone before her, like her husband and everyone else she had known? Stoically, as ever, he answered his own question. *Aye, stoically. Like a good Ulsterwoman. Like a good, church-going Ulsterwoman, isn't that right, Ma?*

Now he was upstairs in the house. Back in his bedroom. He was a wee boy again, tucked up in his bed, safe and cosy and gazing out at the stars. *It's like cartoon land up there, Ma. And I'm like Peter Pan, flying up to the stars. If I could just reach out and touch that big one...*

Chapter One

Edinburgh, 1985

The computer printout occupying the centre of Dan McKay's desk was several inches thick. Although much of the company's operations had been computerised by then, most of its staff still wouldn't have known what to do with the printout – or with any printout, for that matter. To them, those reams of continuous green and white banded sheets overprinted with columns of figures were foreign and unintelligible; "piano paper with squiggles" was how they usually described the sheets.

But Dan was different. Dan had embraced computerisation when it came along a few years before. He had become a champion of the new technology, one of a handful of younger employees to help the organisation join the great digital revolution and enter the so-called enlightened age of the computer.

The reward for his efforts was to have been put in charge of the company's newly automated revenues system, with responsibility for the collection of rent to the value of more than fifty million pounds annually. That responsibility, in turn, earned him a place on the senior management team of the Housing Management Department of the Scottish National Housing Company, the giant quango which owned more than one hundred thousand houses located throughout the length and breadth of Scotland.

Dan considered himself a self-made man. He had joined the company when he was nineteen, having recently flunked his first year at university. He started as a junior clerical officer, the lowest of the low, whose primary duties were filing and making tea. But now, at thirty-five, he had position and influence, with a salary to match. He was immensely proud of what he had achieved. And he was quick to tell anyone who would listen that he had risen from tea-boy to senior manager through simple hard work and sheer determination.

While Dan's career at the SNHC was successful and stable at that time, the same could not be said of his private life. Less than a year earlier, the latter had changed irrevocably when his wife left him without warning, taking with her their three children, the youngest of whom was still a toddler. It transpired that throughout the whole of their twelve-year marriage she had been conducting an affair with an old school friend and had finally decided to go and live with him, her inducement to abandon the marriage after all those years being the imminent prospect of her secret lover inheriting a sizeable hotel business from his elderly parents.

What followed for Dan was a period of utter misery, punctuated by bouts of rage, despair and drunkenness. But slowly, gradually, he emerged from the misery to put his world back in order. He found a solicitor, through whom divorce proceedings were put in motion, a sum of alimony was agreed and regular access to his children was arranged. Then he bought a flat – a bachelor pad – back in his home town, a few miles outside of Edinburgh. And he began to build a new social life – one that was centred on his local pub, but a social life nonetheless.

Where other men might have been broken by the devastation of losing everything they held dear in such a brutal fashion, Dan had survived – though not unscarred. He had developed a pathological mistrust of relationships with women that threatened to go beyond one-night stands. There were words the lawyers had used, words of shame, that still made him seethe with anger: for twelve long years, he had existed as a *cuckold*, while his wife, his so-called partner for life, in whom he had entrusted all his hopes and dreams and fears, had been fornicating with her *paramour*. And even now there were times when he would wake up in a cold sweat in the middle of the night and wonder if the children really were his.

Dan had much to thank his job for; without it, he wouldn't have survived nearly so well. When all else around him was disintegrating, his work had remained constant and solid, a rock he could cling to. Sure, there had been times when his grasp slipped – when the killer hangover or the bout of depression proved too much to bear – but those had been momentary lapses. He had persevered with the job and kept himself focused on it – and he had prospered as a result. Now, those lapses well behind him, he was at the top of his game, completely in control. And that wodge of "piano paper" lying on his desk would help to keep him in control. He was looking forward to poring over the "squiggles" it contained, relishing the figures that should confirm all was well with the complex computer system he had set up: *his* system, his baby.

Dan had hardly begun to examine the figures when there was a light knock at the door of his office, followed by the entrance of two visitors. Shrugging off the disappointment of having to postpone his enjoyment of the printout, he stood up and smiled.

"Morning, boss," he addressed the older visitor.

"Good morning, Dan," replied Les Thomson in his West of Scotland drawl, sounding weary.

Les was the Director of the Housing Management Department, a man in his late fifties, who looked older and always sounded weary. In fact, Les's whole demeanour – the grindingly slow voice that was almost a whine, the slight stoop when he walked, the plodding gait – exuded weariness. He had joined the SNHC back in the early Fifties, when it owned only a couple of thousand houses, and he had risen through the ranks as it had grown in size. He had experienced much change in the organisation. But it seemed now that he had grown tired of change: tired of the constant stream of new policies that had to be implemented at the behest of the Thatcher Government; tired of always having to compete with his fellow-Directors for the resources needed to introduce those policies; tired of all this computer malarkey. In short, Les was more than ready for retirement.

"Can I introduce our latest member of staff?" he continued, placing a hand on the shoulder of the younger visitor. "This is James Boston. Our very own Research Officer. James is from Belfast. He comes to us straight from the Northern Ireland Housing Executive, where he's been doing great things, by all accounts. And I'm sure he's going to do great things for us as well."

James stepped towards Dan's outstretched hand.

"Nice to meet you, Dan," he grinned.

"And you, too."

They shook hands across Dan's desk. Dan reckoned that James was in his mid to late twenties, quite a few years younger than himself. He also noted that James's handshake was firm and dry; he hoped his was the same.

The two men were very different in appearance. James was easily six feet and powerfully built. *A rugby player*, Dan thought immediately. Dan was lucky if he reached five feet six, his wiry frame owing a lot to his current bachelor existence. James was clean-shaven and short-haired, whereas Dan wore a full beard and hair that hadn't been cut for a while, the latter also owing much to his bachelorhood. Ditto, Dan's open-necked checked shirt and casual trousers, contrasting with James's shirt and tie and suit, although it seemed to Dan that the suit could have done with a bit of a press.

"James is doing the rounds of the senior staff today," drawled Les. "He's trying to build up a clearer picture of everyone's research requirements. He'll be putting together a list of proposals, which we'll attempt to prioritise at the next management team meeting. I've no doubt you'll have a lot to go on the list, Dan."

"I certainly will, boss."

"Okay, James, I'll leave you with Dan for the time being. Just make your way back to my office whenever you're finished here."

"I won't tire him out too much, boss, honest," Dan laughed.

Les smiled at both men and closed the door softly behind him. He sighed as he trudged back along the corridor. Obtaining agreement to the new post of Research Officer had been another epic struggle at the Board, yet another drain on him. The Chief Executive and the other Directors couldn't or wouldn't grasp the value to his Department of a dedicated research function, and, as usual, he had great difficulty making them understand. But, also as usual, he had persisted and got there in the end.

Les sighed again. Now he had the added worry of finding a budget to go along with the new post. He *would* find the money, though; he'd put a budget together somehow. Research – good, solid research – was vital to the survival of his Department in an environment where Thatcher and her Ministers were questioning every housing policy going and demanding innovation. All his senior staff claimed to have big research needs, of course. The problem was that their suggestions for research projects were usually nebulous and not very well thought out. Except for Dan, that is, whose ideas always seemed more precise and better developed. So it was no coincidence that he had chosen Dan as the first port of call for James today.

Les had a lot of respect for Dan. Although Dan was often unconventional and sometimes too ready to speak his mind, he was also a sharp-minded thinker and always full of ideas – *practical* ideas. He was a real asset to the Department. When Dan first joined the company, he had reminded Les of himself as a young man: quick on the uptake, keen to learn and progress. But that was before conscription and Palestine. That was before all the eagerness was knocked out of him.

Just as they had done almost every day for the best part of forty years, memories of his time as a fresh-faced conscript with the British Army in Palestine in 1947 came unbidden to Les. And they brought with them a reminder of how much he hated the Jews. Not all Jews, of course – he wasn't even remotely anti-Semitic – but some Jews. And one in particular. The one they called Menachem Begin, until recently the Israeli Prime Minister and now, God forbid, a revered elderly statesman in the Middle East. But back then Begin was the leader of a terrorist gang, a bunch of killers who targeted the British administration in Palestine and who succeeded in maiming and murdering not a few British civilians and soldiers.

Les sighed once more as he opened the door to his own office. Those fear-filled months he spent in Palestine were the worst period of his life. Even now, he couldn't believe that Begin had never paid for his crimes. And he was sure that the day he realised Begin would get off scot-free was the day his jaundiced outlook on the world, his weariness of everything, began.

By the time Les was back at his desk, Dan and James had taken seats at the meeting table in Dan's office. James had pulled out a small notebook and a pen from a side-pocket of his jacket. Dan didn't intend to take notes, so he sat with nothing in front of him. Besides, the things he needed to relay to the new Research Officer were already firm in his head.

"Yer man Les seems like a really nice guy," James began the conversation.

The voice surprised Dan. The Belfast accent wasn't at all similar to the harsh, intimidating one he was used to hearing on the television and radio from the likes of Ian Paisley. It was much softer, with a bit of a lilt, more akin to his mother's brogue. But it was a voice he would come to despise.

"Aye, he's certainly that. A nice guy," Dan agreed. "But sometimes too nice, too soft for his own good. Especially when it comes to the Board. That lot can be real bullying bastards. To be honest, I don't think Les has much fight left in him. I'm sure he would jump at the chance of early retirement if it was offered to him tomorrow."

James nodded. "Yeah, I have to admit his heart doesn't seem to be in it. Earlier on, when he was briefing me about the structure of the Department and where I fitted into it, it was as if he was just going through the motions."

It was Dan's turn to nod. However, realising that he might have said too much already about Les's fragile state of mind, he changed tack.

"Has Les bored you yet about Palestine and Begin?"

James had a ready smile. "Jeez," he laughed, "it was the very first thing he told me. And he's convinced that the situation in Palestine back then was comparable to what's going on in Northern Ireland now. That's rubbish, of course, but I just agreed with him. People over here don't understand what the Troubles are all about."

People over here don't understand. Dan had heard those same words spoken recently in a pub in Edinburgh by a loud-mouthed South African trying to defend apartheid in his country. He knew much more about the Troubles than James imagined. And he tended to concur with Les's Palestine comparison, particularly where the role of the British Army was concerned. But he decided to hold his peace – at least for the time being. He had already guessed that James wasn't a Catholic like him.

"Aye, right," was all he said before changing tack again. "Les circulated your CV to us. A PhD from Queen's University. Very impressive. So what do we call you then? Doctor James? Or Doc Jim?"

James grimaced. "Not Doctor, please not. I couldn't abide those pretentious people at Queen's who insisted on being addressed that way. Anyway, for some daft reason that I still can't explain, the PhD is in Geography and doesn't really mean much – not in a housing company, for sure. Back in the Housing Executive everyone just called me Jimbo. Jimbo as opposed to Jim to distinguish me from all the other Jims in the place. I'm sure there are plenty of Jims here as well."

"Quite a few, aye. Jimbo it is then. So how are you liking Edinburgh, Jimbo? Settling in okay?"

"Great so far. With the help of a very generous relocation payment from the company, we've bought ourselves a lovely wee house out in Joppa. And my wife – she's a nurse – starts her new job at the Western General today. Everything's coming together, touch wood. I've even applied to join the local rugby club. I played a lot of rugby back home. Are you interested in the game yourself?"

Dan laughed. "Not me. I'm more of a football person, kind of.

Watching, not playing, though. I haven't kicked a ball since I was a teenager. But good luck with your application."

Jimbo smiled and cleared his throat before continuing. "Aye, we're really delighted to be here. A different world is an understatement. It's poison over there, you know – and getting worse by the day. The young folk are leaving in droves. There's just no future for them in the Province – it's dying. Most of our friends have already left. So we decided to join the exodus."

"I'm sure you've made the right decision," Dan replied weakly. Then, as was his nature, he decided to confront the elephant in the room. "I'll be straight with you, Jimbo. My mother came from Eire. County Cavan. Border country. Her father was a lieutenant-colonel in the IRA, the old IRA, under Michael Collins, so I was brought up with tales of the Easter Rising, the Black and Tans, and all that."

He paused. *Christ*, he thought, *I've told that story so many times it must have sounded like a rehearsed speech.*

"Anyway," he continued, "I'm a strong supporter of what the Civil Rights movement was trying to achieve in Northern Ireland back in the Sixties when the Troubles began, but I don't for one second condone the actions of the IRA, the new lot. In fact, the day my mother raised her fists in the air and cheered when it was announced on TV that the first British soldier had been murdered by the IRA was the day I left home. I was nineteen at the time, and I just couldn't make her understand that that young soldier could have been one of my pals – or even me, for fuck's sake."

Jimbo was smiling. Smiling because he had correctly spotted a trace of the Republic in Dan's accent. Smiling because he could relax now. *Danny Boy's a Taig, all right. But he's no threat. I met lots of Taigs at Queen's and then at the Housing Executive, didn't I? And got on with them all? I can work with this one, for sure.*

"Aye, feelings will always run deep across the island of Ireland," he said, still smiling. "Thanks for letting me know where you stand, Dan."

With the elephant now well and truly banished from the room, Dan felt he could relax as well. It was time for business.

"A tenants' satisfaction survey," he began. "I suppose that's what everyone, me included, will tell you is the Department's biggest research requirement. The Government has been pressing us for ages to get one done. I hear satisfaction surveys are all the rage among housing authorities down in England. But I haven't a clue how you'd go about organising one."

Jimbo's smile widened. This stuff was like bread and butter to him.

"I've been doing satisfaction surveys at the Housing Executive till they're coming out of my ears. Once you know the basics, they're pretty straightforward, really. You start by putting a questionnaire together. Then you draw a sample of the tenants to be given the questionnaire. The best way of getting responses to the questionnaire is by interviewing tenants direct in their homes. That way will also give you the highest quality survey results. Much better quality than sending the questionnaires in the post, for example."

Dan looked puzzled. "Right," he nodded, "but it all sounds pretty expensive. I don't know how many tenants the Housing Executive has, but we have something like a hundred thousand. Wouldn't you need to draw a massive sample of them? And who would do the interviewing? We've got houses in every corner of Scotland. Would you have to train up a whole army of staff to go round the country and knock on doors?"

Jimbo's smile turned into a laugh. "No, Dan, it doesn't need to be too expensive, honestly. That crappy Geography doctorate of mine might not be of much use here, but the one useful thing it has given me is a detailed knowledge of sampling techniques. It's all very scientific, and there are formulae involved, but the first main thing to note is that as long as it's selected on a random and systematic basis the sample you draw for any survey doesn't have to be big. With a sample of just under four hundred, for example, you can obtain pretty accurate survey results. The margin of error on any survey percentage would be no more than plus or minus five per cent."

It was Dan's turn to laugh. "Apart from the fact that we could get away with a fairly small sample, you realise that most of that went right over my head, pal? But a sample of as little as four hundred, though? That's amazing."

"And it gets better. The next main thing to remember is that the four hundred remains constant notwithstanding the size of the population – that's the total number of tenants, in your case – being surveyed. Whether you're surveying the Scottish National Housing Company's tenants only or the whole of the population of Scotland, the same size of sample will be sufficient. With a few exceptions, it's the size of the sample that matters, not the size of the population."

Dan signified that he understood, allowing Jimbo to continue.

"Now, very often when you do surveys you'll go for a bigger sample than four hundred. That's not just because you want more accurate results overall, but because you want a breakdown of the results for different population groups. You might want to analyse the findings by age group, for example, or by region. Let's say you want a regional analysis for four regions – north, south, west and east..."

"Okay," said Dan, simply to indicate that he was still taking it in.

"...then you'd select a reasonably sized sample – enough to produce what are called *significant* results – for each region. If you went for, say, two hundred and fifty in each case, you'd need a total sample of one thousand. Which is a bit of a magic number, really. If you ever look at any of the national surveys conducted by MORI and NOP, you'll see that the findings are always based on a sample of one thousand..."

Dan threw his hands up in mock surrender. "Christ, Jimbo!" he laughed again. "You certainly know your stuff, sir. You've got me convinced, anyway. And I think you've just answered my earlier question about who would carry out the survey. Presumably, we'd have to pay the likes of MORI or NOP to do it."

"Aye, you could, I suppose. As I understand it, both companies run nationwide fieldwork forces in Scotland, so I've no doubt they could easily send out a team of interviewers across the country. The problem is, though, they're in the top echelon of market research agencies in the UK, if not in Europe, and they'd cost a bomb – more than the SNHC could afford, if what Les says is anything to go by. Naw, we'd need to look at other agencies, cheaper alternatives. I'm sure there will be some. Over in the Province, there were two or three companies we used on a regular basis. Latterly, we were using a small Belfast-based outfit by the name of Market Surveys Northern Ireland. Funnily enough, the chap who owns it, Neville Brown, recently moved to Scotland to set up a company in Glasgow. Yer man Neville is a great guy, by the way, but he doesn't have much of an imagination, so he's calling the company Market Surveys Scotland."

Jimbo stopped there to chuckle at his own joke.

"Anyway," he continued, "I'm due to catch up with Neville later this week, so we'll see if his new company is going to be in a position to tender for the tenant satisfaction survey – if the survey does go ahead, that is..."

"Well, good luck with that. But listen, don't be put off too much by what Les says. He's always Mister Doom and Gloom when it comes to spending money. All the senior management team are totally behind the survey. More importantly, the Government wants it done. So it's pretty much in the bag. It *will* go ahead, trust me. And don't forget when the time comes that I'll have a few things of my own to be included in the questionnaire."

"You'll be first on the list of those to be consulted, honest," Jimbo smiled, although he still didn't sound completely convinced by Dan's assurance.

"I'm not sure I understood it all, but that survey stuff is fascinating. You learn new things every day. The survey aside, though, I have a few research projects of my own to sound you out about."

Jimbo picked up his pen and opened his notebook. "Fire away," he said.

During the next half-hour, Dan spoke about his proposed projects, while Jimbo took notes and enthusiastically outlined how the projects might be approached. He suggested that a couple of them could involve computer modelling, a technique in which he was also well versed. In each case, the computer model would use a sample of records drawn from Dan's revenues system. In each case, too, the sample would be selected using a method which Jimbo called random probability sampling, the same method he had described earlier for the tenant satisfaction survey. *Random probability sampling.* In the years ahead, those three words would come to dominate the lives of the two men.

"It's been a pleasure doing business with you," Dan declared as they stood up at the end of the meeting and shook hands – the same firm, dry handshakes given and received as before.

"Ditto," Jimbo agreed and added, "I think my biggest problem will be in securing a proper budget for the post. According to Les, a budget hasn't been agreed yet. Apart from the satisfaction survey, you'll see from our own discussions that at the very least I'll need to get my hands on a good PC and a shitload of analysis software for the computer modelling. And maybe some clerical help in due course..."

"Don't worry about all that, Jimbo. Les said you had been invited to the next senior management team meeting. My advice is to do your sums beforehand. Come along to the meeting not just with a list of proposed research projects, but with a note of what they're likely to cost. Set your own budget figure. I, for one, will be there to ensure your figure is agreed."

"Thanks, Dan," Jimbo beamed as he opened the door to leave.

"Oh, by the way," Dan caught him, "a crowd of us usually make our way to the West End Wine Bar after work on a Friday. It's just round the corner from here. No' the most salubrious of places, but it does us okay. A wee home from home, if you like. You're welcome to join us any time. I'll even buy you a pint, Doc."

Jimbo beamed again and gave a thumbs-up sign. "I'll hold you to that," he said and left the room.

While Dan sat down at his desk and resumed his examination of the printout, Jimbo returned to Les's office feeling rather pleased with the outcome of his first meeting. He had found an ally, someone senior who would support him from the outset. But he had found more than that. There was something about Dan McKay: his sharpness, his confidence, his informality. Taig or not, the wee man was a kindred spirit.

Chapter Two

Edinburgh, 1988

Big change was afoot at the Scottish National Housing Company. At the behest of the Government, the organisation was being restructured – "to make the SNHC leaner, more modern and more responsive to the housing policy challenges of tomorrow", the Housing Minister had proclaimed.

So the management consultants had been brought in. Some departments would disappear under the revised structure recommended by the consultants; others would merge; and yet others would be newly created. Heads were rolling at the top of the company, to be replaced by new, unfamiliar and invariably younger heads. And the new heads were being charged with the organisation of their shiny new departments, bringing in their own management consultants, if necessary.

It was a time of upheaval for everyone and a time of opportunity or threat. Some staff would have to re-apply for their own jobs, some were being told to apply for new jobs elsewhere in the organisation, and many would end up with no job at all and a redundancy package instead. While words like "modernisation" and "streamlining" were being bandied about by those on high, most staff suspected that this was simply another Government-dictated, cost-cutting exercise, so characteristic of the Thatcher era, and that there would be laughter for some and tears for many before it was all over.

On that Friday afternoon in the midst of the reorganisation, it was little wonder that hardly any work had been carried out in the SNHC's headquarters, a row of converted Georgian townhouses on the western fringe of Edinburgh's New Town. Hushed, worried conversations between staff had been held everywhere – in people's rooms, out in the corridors, huddled round photocopiers and on the stairs. It was little wonder, too, that after the offices closed a good number of those conversations continued in the dimness of the West End Wine Bar. Located in a basement below a shop a mere stone's throw from the headquarters, the place had seen better days. It had actually operated as a pukka wine bar back in the Seventies, when such establishments were in vogue. Now it was a drinking howff, frequented for the most part by SNHC staff.

By five o'clock, the bar was already half-filled with SNHC people. But they weren't behaving like the usual noisy, chattering Friday evening crowd, out to celebrate the end of a working week. They were quieter and more earnest. And not one of them had sought to stick money in the jukebox. It was as if the subdued tone of the conversations across in the offices had followed them over and permeated the place.

Dan and Jimbo were at a table on their own in a corner of the bar. Dan had a pint of lager in front of him; it would be the first of many before the night was out. It was Friday, after all, and his place of work – the place he had devoted the best part of twenty years to – was falling apart. What better excuses could he have?

Jimbo sat with his customary two bottles of Becks and a schooner glass; he loathed the modern habit of drinking straight from the neck of the bottle, so a glass was mandatory. If his few visits to the bar in the last year were anything to go by, he would finish the two beers and head off, first to the gym and then to meet up with his girlfriend, Sally, and go for a meal. It had been a long time since he had settled down with Dan and other SNHC colleagues for a Friday night session in the bar.

Sally also worked for the company, as a clerical officer in the Finance Department. Considerably younger than Jimbo and pretty, she had moved in with him a while ago. Dan didn't have much time for her. She had one of those shrill, wee lassie voices he couldn't abide. The way she clung to Jimbo, her "handsome hunk", in public nauseated him. And although nothing much ever seemed to go on in her brain – she always reminded him of *Pretty Vacant*, the Sex Pistols song – he suspected she was a bit of a schemer.

Dan often wondered what had happened to Jimbo's wife. After their first meeting three years earlier, Jimbo hadn't spoken of her to him again, not even to mention her name. Dan was left to assume that, not having found life in Edinburgh to her liking, she had returned to Northern Ireland. He thought the mystery surrounding her departure was typical of Jimbo: forever keen to grill people about their personal circumstances, but never willing to divulge anything about his own.

Dan's private life had also undergone much change during those three years. Having eventually (and with no little difficulty) overcome his unease about entering into another long-term relationship, he, too, now had a regular girlfriend, and she, too, was a good few years younger than him. Alma had once been employed by him across the road. A divorcee who had returned to full-time education, she was currently at university studying for a degree in accountancy. She had her own flat in Edinburgh, which he had recently moved into, having sold his one. Away from his hometown and his pub-dominated, often lonely existence there, he had found a kind of serenity in his new life with Alma. But it was a serenity increasingly under threat from the turmoil of the reorganisation.

As usual on a Friday evening, Alma was due to come down to the bar later on. She and Dan would then sit and drink and laugh (and no doubt discuss the reorganisation) with a bunch of Dan's friends, after which they would go for something to eat, probably to the Chinese restaurant opposite the bar. In the meantime, Dan was eager to hear what Jimbo had to tell him. Unusually, it was Jimbo – with important news to share, he had hinted – who had suggested that the pair of them should meet in the bar so early. Before the talking could begin, however, Dan sipped his pint and waited while Jimbo completed his customary pre-drinking ritual.

Jimbo took off his suit jacket, folded it over so that the lining was on show, folded it again in two and placed it carefully on top of his gym bag, which he had set down on the floor at the side of his chair. Then he straightened his tie, flattened down his shirt front and yanked at each of his shirt sleeves in turn to ensure the cuffs rose above his wrists. Finally, he poured one of the bottles into his glass, raised the glass in salute, took a large mouthful of beer and gave out a sigh of satisfaction.

"Nectar, so it is," he said.

As he watched the performance, Dan noted that Jimbo's suits were more frequently pressed than they used to be. Likewise, his (invariably white) shirts were crisper and fresher. Overall, he appeared much better groomed these days. Dan wondered if the sharper look was Sally's doing, but immediately dismissed the notion.

Nor, he was certain, did Sally have anything to do with Jimbo's frequent visits to the gym. The visits had begun shortly after Jimbo ended his association with the local rugby club. That was less than a year after his arrival in Edinburgh and long before he met Sally. Jimbo had never elaborated on his reasons for leaving the rugby club, but Dan suspected that there had been some kind of falling out with others in the club – which was not surprising, he supposed, given Jimbo's track record since.

Whatever Jimbo's original motivation for joining the gym, Dan had to admit that the results of his sessions there were very noticeable. His physique had always been broad and muscular, like the archetypal rugby player, but now his shoulders were even wider, his neck thicker and his chest bigger; in fact, his whole upper torso seemed to strain against the fabric of his shirt.

Dan recalled the time there in the bar a few months back when a weedy, red-haired accountant, who happened to be Sally's boss, jokingly accused Jimbo of wearing shirts that were too small so that he could show off his muscles to the women. As usual, Jimbo didn't take the joke well and left the bar shortly afterwards, no doubt having marked down Sally's boss as yet another sworn enemy.

"Cheers," called Jimbo, raising his glass again and interrupting Dan's train of thought.

Dan raised his own glass. "Aye, cheers, Jimbo," he replied. "And thanks for the pint, pal."

Jimbo looked round the bar. "It's pretty busy in here already," he remarked, "even for a Friday."

"Aye, well, folk have a lot to talk about, I suppose, with the reorganisation and all that. Did you hear the latest about Les, by the way? Gone, apparently. Early retirement with immediate effect. No farewells. No leaving do. No' even a gold watch after all those years. Just gone, vanished, as if he had never existed. It's fuckin' brutal, this process, you ken. And look what they're putting in his place. Fuckin' laughable, I tell you."

Dan stopped to take a mouthful of his drink. Then he resumed, climbing on his latest hobbyhorse.

"Aye, those fuckin' consultants – *your* consultants, the ones you recommended – have a lot to answer for. They promised at the outset that they would use the results of the psychometric tests to supplement their interviews with the senior staff. But it looks to me as if it's the other way round. They're using the psychometric tests to place people in posts and putting little, if any, weight on the interviews. And, as you well ken, some of the outcomes are bizarre, to say the least. My interview with them was a fuckin' joke, by the way..."

Jimbo smiled and put his hands up in mock-surrender. He had heard the same tirade from Dan a couple of times before. He had also heard the same complaints from others.

"Look," he sighed. "In my role as Research Officer, I was asked to come up with potential management consultants who could help to restructure the Department. And, sure, I recommended those two guys. I knew them because they did a lot of good work for the Housing Executive. As far as I'm concerned, they're a pair of easy-going, down-to-earth Belfast lads who know their stuff inside out."

More like a pair of smooth-talking charlatans, thought Dan, but he kept quiet and let Jimbo finish.

"If the guys are doing things wrong, I don't think it'll be their fault. I think it'll be because they've been told to cut corners and speed up the process. Anyway, I can't really comment on what's going on. As you know, not being a member of senior management, I'm not part of the process." He paused. "Which is really what I came to talk to you about tonight."

Dan wanted to tell Jim that his two countrymen didn't have a clue and were cutting corners of their own volition. He said instead, "Sorry, Jimbo, I didn't mean to launch into all that. And I know you've listened to me sounding off about that pair before. I'm dying to hear your news, so please spill the beans, pal."

Jimbo finished off the beer in his glass and poured the second bottle of Becks into it before beginning.

"Well, no surprise that I'm also bothered about the reorganisation. I've been with the company for over three years now, and during that time, with a lot of support from yourself and some of the other senior staff, I've managed to build up my wee section – and, I hope, a good reputation..."

"Definitely."

"As you know, until the reorganisation was announced, it was pretty much on the cards that my post would be elevated to senior management level, thanks again to you and a few others. The problem is I can't see that happening now – at least, not in the foreseeable future. So I got speaking the other day to Neville Brown. Remember him? I'm sure I've mentioned Neville before. His company, Market Surveys Scotland, did the big tenant satisfaction survey for us."

"Aye, I remember you telling me about him."

"He's a great guy is Neville. Bald as a coot, but younger than me. And running his own business. Well, anyway, yer man Neville asks me what kind of salary I'd be looking for if I did get a more senior position in the SNHC. So I tell him thirty grand. And immediately, without blinking, he says he'll double that figure if I join Market Surveys Scotland instead.

And he'll throw in a car. And shares in the company. With the prospect of a full partnership in time."

Dan's mouth had dropped open. "Fuckin' hell, Jimbo."

"Aye, he wants me to come in and manage the company's public sector research, doing surveys for Councils and the like across Scotland. There's definitely a big market for the work. I know, for example, that every Council Housing Department wants their own tenant satisfaction survey carried out. And that's just one Council Department out of many. It's the tip of the iceberg, so it is."

"Fuckin' hell," Dan could only repeat.

"It goes without saying that I've been thinking a lot about Neville's offer. Whether I can trust the guy – he could talk the hind legs off a donkey, so he could. And whether there really is a sustainable job there – it is the private sector, after all. Then the news today about Les put the tin lid on it. Any support I might have had at Board level has gone now. So I've made up my mind. I'll be submitting my resignation on Monday. Apart from Neville – and Sal, of course – you're the first to know. But could you keep it under your hat until it becomes official?"

Dan laughed. "In case you change your mind over the weekend, you mean? Don't be daft. It's the offer of a lifetime, pal, and you'd be off your head to turn it down. Seriously, though, I'm really pleased for you. And don't worry, I'll keep shtum."

"You're right, it's a bit of a no-brainer, I suppose," Jimbo shrugged. "But it's a big step to be taking nonetheless. I just wanted time to think it through."

"Well, good fuckin' luck to you, Jimbo. You never know, I might be joining you in the private sector in the not too distant future. I'm seriously thinking about leaving as well, maybe going into consultancy on my own. Housing consultancy, that is – *not* management consultancy. At my so-called interview this week, I said that I wanted to do something in policy or strategy, but those two cunts wouldn't listen. They kept repeating that my psycho-fuckin'-metric test showed that my key strength was as an operational manager – my operational score was so high it was nearly off the page, apparently – and therefore they would be recommending me for an operational post in the restructured Department. It didn't matter what *I* wanted to do, which I thought was the whole purpose of the interview. So it looks like I'm going to end up doing what I'm doing just now, but probably with a boss who knows fuck all about–"

Dan stopped himself in mid-sentence.

"Apologies once more for going off on one, Jimbo," he continued sheepishly. "This discussion is meant to be about you, not me. Are you up for celebrating? Or at least are you up for another beer?"

"No, honest, Dan. I'm trying to keep my head clear for now. There should be plenty of time for celebrating once my news is public. Anyway, I'm due to meet Sal up town later on. But I'm going to hit the gym first."

"To pump some more iron, eh?"

"Aye, something like that," Jimbo smiled.

He finished his second beer and reached down for his jacket.

"It looks like you have a lot to consider yourself," he said, standing up and putting on the jacket. "Housing consultancy, you said. I know a couple of lads from the Housing Executive who went off to do that. I'm not sure how they got on, though. It can be a dicey business, I believe, so you'll need to think carefully about it."

"Oh, I will, Jimbo, I will. Meantime, enjoy the gym and don't forget the Johnson's."

Jimbo looked perplexed. "Johnson's?"

"Aye, Johnson's baby oil. For rubbing on your pecs."

Jimbo laughed as he picked up his gym bag.

"Fuck off, McKay," he waved and left the bar, nodding to a group of SNHC people as he passed them at the door.

Dan sat back and lit a cigarette. He had refrained from smoking until then less out of politeness to his colleague, but more because he didn't want to put up with Jimbo's rigmarole of blowing air up his nostrils every few seconds and waving his hand like a fan in front of his mouth. Not for the first time he wondered where that particular little performance of his had come from. Back in the early days, Jimbo didn't seem to bother about people smoking in his company. But somewhere along the line he had developed what amounted to a pathological hatred of the habit. Dan shrugged. *Ah, well,* he thought, *if you can't stand the smoke, you shouldn't come into pubs, pal.*

Looking round the bar, he spotted a group of his drinking buddies seated in another corner. It didn't surprise him that none of them had ventured near his and Jimbo's table, not even just to say hello. The fact of the matter was that the majority of SNHC people who frequented the bar were wary of Jimbo and tended to avoid him. There had been too many occasions, too many Friday nights, when Jimbo had become fiercely argumentative with others. Most of the arguments had been over trivial matters to do with work or sport or music, but a few had become very serious. Like the time Jimbo argued with Brian Kelly that the Belfast Blitz in 1941, although hardly known about elsewhere in the UK, had been far more devastating than the Luftwaffe's bombing raids along the River Clyde, also in 1941. Brian, who originated from Clydebank and who had lost relatives in the blitz of that town, found himself virtually under attack by Jimbo. The poor man had left the bar almost in tears and, as far as Dan was aware, had never set foot in the place again.

Dan shook his head at the memory of that incident. It had all been so unnecessary. But that was the thing about Jimbo when it came to arguments; the arguments rapidly turned into competitions, in which he had to try to browbeat his opponents into submitting, with no quarter given. On the rare occasions when he failed, he would slope off in a huff like a spoilt kid, never again to acknowledge, let alone converse with, those he had lost to. Which is exactly what happened when he attempted to argue politics with Alma the first time they met. Now the two of them hardly spoke to each other.

Dan reckoned that the argumentative Jimbo had manifested himself about the same time as the anti-smoking Jimbo. He often wondered what had triggered him to become so intolerant. He was certain it wasn't drink – Jimbo could begin an argument even before finishing his first beer. No, it had to be something else. Perhaps it all began when his wife left him to return to Belfast, the anger that raged within him finding an outlet through the arguments. Or perhaps he was simply showing his true colours: the true colours of an intolerant, bullying Ulsterman. Whichever was the case, he seemed to have developed a split-personality: one moment the charming, affable Irishman who first joined the SNHC; the next literally seething with aggression.

Despite Jimbo's faults, Dan continued to regard him as a good friend, with whom he had worked well over the years. He had a lot of respect for Jimbo's intelligence and abilities. And he felt that the feeling was mutual, that there was still a kind of bond between them. They didn't always see eye to eye, of course, especially on matters to do with the Troubles, but he had never been the target of one of Jimbo's bursts of anger. He wished Jimbo every success with his big opportunity, which surely he would grasp come Monday morning.

Meanwhile, he had some anger issues of his own to deal with. This reorganisation business wasn't doing his temper any good. Perhaps a few more pints would help to mellow it. He stubbed out his cigarette, stood up with his pint in his hand and headed towards the other corner. As if on cue, the jukebox blared into life.

Chapter Three

Glasgow, 1989

Neville Brown stepped up to the front door of the office building, turned to take in the view of the park, glistening green in the early morning sunshine, and decided that life was good.

The building was one of a sweeping terrace of Victorian townhouses built on the crest of the hill overlooking Kelvingrove Park in Glasgow's West End. Neville's company, Market Surveys Scotland, occupied its top floor and attic.

He watched as his partner, Izzy, trudged up the steps towards him, a pile of folders under one arm and their two-year-old Yorkshire terrier nestled in the crook of the other. She was wearing an old denim jacket today over a floral dress that reached down to her ankles.

Very fuckin' Laura Ashley, Neville sneered to himself.

He opened the plate glass door to let her into the office.

"You go on up," he said. "I'm enjoying the sun. It's not often it shines in Glasgow, you know."

"Aye, okay, Nev," Izzy sighed, stooping down to deposit the dog on the ground.

The dog yelped and scampered up the stair. Izzy followed, her low-heeled, scuffed white shoes click-clacking as she ascended.

"Mind now, Nev," she called from the first landing, "Jimbo says he wants to see you this morning. Something urgent. He sounded fair harassed on the phone, so he did."

Neville grunted his acknowledgement. He watched Izzy's progress for a few moments longer before letting go of the door. Then, shaking his head, he turned to face the park and the sun again.

He really wished that Izzy would tidy herself up before coming to the office. He had complained to her countless times about her appearance, but she always said she was too busy pandering to him to bother about herself. All he wanted was a bit of cooked breakfast in the morning. How fuckin' hard was that? His Ma used to do it every day for his Da and him – and she never once looked as dowdy and unkempt.

Dowdy and unkempt, he repeated the words to himself. *Yes, good words to describe Izzy. Jeez, you'd think she'd slept in that frock she's wearing. The hair looks greasy as well. I'll bet it hasn't seen a brush today. And it's more dirty brown than blonde these days. Yes, my dear, the fuckin' roots need doing again!*

Making a mental note to speak to Izzy that night about her roots, Neville closed his eyes and let the sun's rays wash over his face. He tried to think about work, about the tasks he needed to accomplish that day, but, as usual, his mind was wandering. His thoughts had progressed from the specific topic of Izzy's appearance to the subject of women in general – his favourite subject, in fact. He wondered why it was that all the women in Belfast wanted to dye their hair blonde. It had gotten so that you never knew the true colour of their hair until their knickers were off. Even the Taig women were at it.

His mind was off again. *Aye, there's me turned thirty now and I've yet to shag a Taig. And it's not been for the want of trying. The Neville Brown charm doesn't seem to impress that lot. But maybe one day. I'd love to fuck a red-haired one, so I would. The skin so pale you can see through it. Freckles everywhere. And that red bush. The fiery bush, just like in the Bible...*

The stirring of an erection forced him to open his eyes and try once more to concentrate on work matters. With Izzy's reminder still ringing in his ears, he figured the business of Jimbo wanting to see him – urgently, by all accounts – was at the top of the list. That was odd, though. Just the day before, he and Jimbo, the only two shareholders of Market Surveys Scotland, had sat down with Izzy, the Company Secretary, to go over the draft accounts for last financial year. It had all been very positive. The turnover had virtually doubled over the twelve months. And MSS had made its biggest profit since he started it four years ago. Not a massive sum, he had to admit, but big enough to pay Jimbo and himself handsome dividends and plough the rest back into the business. Even more positive were their projections for this financial year. All the signs were that they would outperform last year – and by a wide margin. *Fuck, the place up there's going like a fair, so it is!*

He couldn't help but grin. Persuading Jimbo to join the company just over a year ago now was probably the shrewdest business move he would ever make. Up until then, he had been chipping away at the private sector, winning mostly smallish contracts from local ad agencies. To tell the truth, he wasn't making much of a name for MSS and was growing jaded as a result. But Jimbo changed all that when he brought in a shitload of public sector jobs. Every one of those jobs was a beauty, too, involving a massive sample of in-home interviews, which was in complete contrast to his own tiddly wee surveys conducted in stores or on the street. The public sector methodology was complicated as fuck, mind you, with things like random probability sampling, sample stratification and weighting – stuff that went right over his head – but methodology was Jimbo's forte. *Our boy has a doctorate, doesn't he? In fact, he's a fuckin' genius!*

Yes, thanks to Doctor Jimbo, he had a spring in his step today. MSS looked like it was going places at long last. And its sister company, Market Surveys Northern Ireland, was ticking over nicely back home. It was a wonderful feeling: knowing that if things went tits up here in Scotland there was always MSNI to fall back on. It wasn't just a bolthole, though; it was his nest egg as well, his insurance for the future. Not only did he own the company, he also owned outright the building it occupied, which happened to be a complete townhouse in the centre of Belfast.

When peace broke out in the Province, which it surely would one day, and property prices shot up as a result, that building would be worth a fortune. His Da had always advised him to stay away from stocks and shares and only invest in bricks and mortar – which is exactly what he had done when he bought MSNI lock, stock and barrel. At the time, he knew sweet fuck all about the market research business, of course, but it wasn't hard to pick up the basics. Besides which a set of damn good staff came with the company, including their bookkeeper, Izzy. It wasn't long before he was shacking up with Izzy. And now, of course, she did the books for both companies, while her brother managed MSNI in his absence.

Having MSNI sitting in the background was a tremendous comfort, right enough. It was a pity that the money for its purchase came from the insurance payout for his Ma and Da after they were wiped out in that terrible pile-up. They were on the M2, on their way back to Belfast from a trip up north, and had just passed Newtownabbey when it happened. *They were only a few miles from home, for fuck's sake!* That was nearly seven years ago now. He was still getting over it, but life had to go on. As their only child, everything they left went to him, including the insurance money. *Ah, well, out of tragedy comes triumph, didn't someone once say?*

Shrugging away the memories of that awful time and the lingering guilt for having prospered in its wake, he returned his thoughts to the positive things that were going on. Life was indeed good. He and Izzy were living comfortably in a grand house just a few miles outside of Glasgow. Business was booming. Profits were being made. And today the sun was shining. Just perfect.

Then, of course, there was the icing on the cake: his *other* career with the Territorial Army. Not long after he took over MSNI, an acquaintance in Belfast recommended the TA as a brilliant way of networking with like-minded businessmen both in the Province and on the mainland. So he applied to join as an Officer, a few words were whispered in the right ear and he was able to go straight in as a Second-Lieutenant. He was now a full Lieutenant. It was in an administrative rather than combat role, but that didn't matter; he was just proud to be serving Queen and country – in whatever the capacity.

He loved the TA. As his acquaintance had predicted, he had built up some solid business contacts through it. It was actually one of those contacts, a property developer from Scotland, who had suggested Glasgow as the ideal place in which to expand his company and who had gone on to help him find an office in the Park area. The TA also paid him a salary – and a damn good one at that. Best of all, though, were the training exercises. They meant that he could legitimately get away from the business (and Izzy) for lengthy periods on a regular basis. As well as carrying out his TA duties on those occasions, he could indulge in what he and his fellow-Officers called the three B's – bonding, boozing and bonking. Naturally, it was the third B that he looked forward to most. It was true what they said about women being attracted to men in uniforms. There he was: bald, skinny, bespectacled and jug-eared, yet he had lost count of the number of women who had virtually dropped their knickers at his feet. He had shagged them up against walls in dark alleys, across the bonnets of cars and even in cupboards in TA quarters. But he still hadn't shagged a red-haired Taig. He still hadn't partaken of the red bush...

Realising that his mind had gone full circle, he decided it was time to get to work. After a last look at the park, he turned about, entered the building and unhurriedly climbed the stair, whistling as he went. When he reached the fourth floor and walked into the MSS office, he smiled, priding himself in the fact that he wasn't remotely out of breath after the climb. That was an added benefit of the TA: it kept him fit.

"Mornin', gurrls," he shouted as he passed the reception counter, hardly glancing at the three young women, all still in their teens, who sat behind it.

"Mornin', Neville," they chanted in unison.

"Coffee!" Neville demanded as he entered the room adjacent to the reception area. By far the biggest room in the suite, with a large bay window that overlooked the park, it doubled as his office and the company's boardroom. His desk occupied the bay of the window, facing away from it and on to the boardroom table and chairs.

Leaving the door open, he crossed the room, sat down at his desk with a sigh and drummed his fingers on it until Monica, the youngest of the three typists-cum-receptionists, arrived with a mug of coffee in one hand and the morning post in the other.

"Thank you, m'dear," he said when the mug and the post had been set down in front of him. "Is Jimbo around?" he added.

"Aye, he is, Neville. Upstairs in his office. D'ye waant me tae go an' get him fur ye?"

"Nah, it's all right, m'dear. He'll be down soon enough, no doubt."

"Okay, Neville."

He sat back and watched Monica leave the room. *The wee girl is what – sixteen or seventeen? Barely out of school. Still carrying a bit of baby fat, but that'll disappear in no time at all. Another freckle-faced ginger-nut from one of those Taig-infested dumps on the outskirts of the city – Drumchapel or some other shit-hole in Glasgow's equivalent of West Belfast. But another fiery bush in the making, perhaps.*

Get them when they're young. The phrase came unbidden to him. It was his motto when it came to employing clerical staff. He'd take on school leavers – exclusively girls – and pay them the minimum wage. Then he'd slip them a bit of a bonus at Christmas time and on their birthdays. They'd repay him a hundredfold in loyalty. Guaranteed.

Not forgetting the socialising. He'd throw an office party every now and then, inviting all the staff, but not their boyfriends or girlfriends or spouses. No partners: that was the cardinal rule, which meant Izzy was excluded, of course. He'd supply plenty of booze and food – at the company's expense, naturally. Then he'd get the dancing going. And a bit of singing. And the party games – they were his favourite. *That Twister game is a cracker! The positions those supple, wee lassies can get themselves into! And us men so close we're rubbing up against them. Especially that horny Jimbo. And then, in the heat of the night when the drink takes over, there's the chance of a quick grope or more in one of the toilets or in the staff shower. Whoever decided to install that shower along there was a fuckin' genius! The perfect wee shagging spot. And well-used by both Jimbo and me during the last couple of parties. What you might call being repaid with more than just loyalty.*

So engrossed was he in remembering his exploits in the shower, he almost failed to notice that Monica's small, plump figure had been replaced at the doorway by Jimbo's broad, muscular frame.

"Got a minute?" Jimbo asked brusquely. He was standing in his shirt-sleeves, holding his copy of the draft company accounts and looking like he meant business.

Neville recovered quickly. "Ah, Jimbo!" he exclaimed. "Just been thinking about you, my friend. Come in. Have a seat. I'll come and join you."

After closing the door and thereby signifying that he wanted a private discussion, Jimbo sat at the boardroom table, placed the draft accounts in front of him and opened them at the page showing the Profit and Loss Account. Neville carried his coffee mug over to the table and sat opposite Jimbo. Recognising that trouble was afoot, he spoke first. It was his way of trying to forestall any nastiness, which he hated and which he'd run a mile from if he could.

"That was a tremendous meeting yesterday, wasn't it? It's given me a real spring in my step today, so it has. Knowing that the company is going places at last. And you're the key to that, Jimbo. I'm sure it won't be long before we're looking at your salary again. And maybe seeing about a better car for you. And I know I keep saying this – that twenty per cent shareholding of yours might be worth nothing now, but a few years from now..."

"That's what I want to speak to you about, Neville. Not about the shares or my package; I'm happy with all that. But about the future – the future profit levels, to be precise."

Jimbo stopped and turned the accounts document round so that the Profit and Loss page was directly in front of Neville.

"See that there?" he said, stabbing a figure at the top of the page with his forefinger. "That's the turnover we made last financial year. Now, if I've got my sums right, something like three-quarters of that amount – the lion's share – was down to jobs I brought in from the public sector. Which leaves only about twenty-five per cent that came from your jobs in the private sector."

Neville was growing uneasy. "Sounds right," he mumbled.

"Well, I don't know if you ever noticed, but I was run ragged last year managing the jobs I won. As I keep telling you, clients in the public sector are very demanding, much more so than in the private sector. I've lost count of the number of times I've driven from one end of Scotland to the other. And it isn't getting any better this year either. I don't have a minute to myself. So, really, something's got to give."

"R-right..." Neville sounded nervous.

That little sign of weakness was enough for Jimbo to launch into his plan with more confidence.

"Now, I know that by far the quickest and easiest – and laziest – solution would be to bring someone in to help me. Another research executive, probably. The problem is, though, that my clients want to see me and not some pimply-faced, wet-behind-the-ears trainee executive. The even bigger problem is that we would have to win more work to meet the extra salary. Either that or accept reduced profits, which I'm sure neither of us wants. It's a vicious circle, you see, Neville. I think it's called chasing turnover to feed the staff. And I think it's what's been happening in the company up until now."

As he spoke, Jimbo's voice seemed to grow louder, his face harder and his posture more threatening. Neville hadn't experienced this version of Jimbo before. Like a rabbit caught in the headlights, he could only sit and watch and listen.

"So I've been giving some thought to what can be done to make life easier for myself – and to boost our profits at the same time. I've come up with a two-pronged attack. The first step, which I think we can implement immediately, is to sort out our pricing policy.

"In the public sector, as you know, it's competitive tendering all the way. Which means that for every contract I tender for I have to compete with other agencies. Invariably, the competition includes the big boys – MORI, in particular, who are very strong in that sector. Now, there's no question that the four City Councils will always go for the big boys – they want an established name to front their surveys and they have the budgets to pay for that name – so I haven't had any success there. It's a different matter among the smaller Councils, though. They seem to be suffering much more than the Cities from the continued squeeze on their funding by Central Government, making them more cost-conscious and therefore more willing to give cheaper, less established companies a chance. And that's where I've been picking up contracts left, right and centre. What I've managed to establish, however, is that where we've been successful our prices haven't just been lower than the nearest unsuccessful company – they've been lower by a long chalk. I reckon, therefore, that I could increase our prices by ten or fifteen per cent, perhaps as much as twenty per cent in a few cases, and still win the same number of jobs. And remember, even a ten per cent price increase would mean adding ten per cent to the bottom line."

Jimbo paused to make sure Neville was still following him before he carried on. Neville responded by grinning and nodding enthusiastically; he was beginning to relax again.

"Which brings us to the private sector. There isn't any other way of saying this, Neville, without it sounding insulting, but as far as I can gather most of your clients regard MSS as a cheap and cheerful alternative to a quality market research agency. If they don't have the money to spend, they'll go to you. But if they want to pay for a bit of quality and finesse, they'll go elsewhere."

In spite of the *cheap and cheerful* jibe, Neville continued to grin and nod.

"Again, therefore, I'm suggesting a hike in the private sector prices of between ten and twenty per cent. I know such a strategy would be a bit of a gamble, but I think it would help to change the bargain-basement image of MSS among your clients. And, once again, it would add to the bottom line."

Inwardly, Neville breathed a huge sigh of relief. Sticking up the prices was easy. And there hadn't been any nastiness at all!

Half-laughing, he spoke at last, "I have no problem whatsoever with what you're proposing, Jimbo. As ever, you're absolutely correct on all counts. We're far too cheap and should do something about that. And we should do it with immediate effect. Just like I was saying to myself earlier on, you're a fuckin' genius, my boy!"

"I'm glad you agree," said Jimbo, the seriousness of his expression unchanged, "because you're not going to be so happy about the next part of the strategy."

Neville's heart sank. He was back staring into the headlights, unable to move.

Jimbo stabbed at another figure on the Profit and Loss Account, this one lower down the page. "You see that sum there? It's what we're paying out for staff and it's where most of our profits are going. It actually accounts for something like eighty per cent of our total overheads, which I think is far too high a proportion and has to be reduced if we want to make some real profits.

"Now, don't get me wrong, I have no difficulty with the majority of the staff. The folk in Field and Data Processing are all doing a grand job, as are the girls at reception. Where I do have a problem is the so-called Executive team. We're forking out for three execs at the moment. None of them does anything for me, so they must be working for you. To be honest, I haven't a clue what the fuck they do. The two young lads aren't being paid much, so you'd probably want to keep them, but I really do wonder if you're getting value for money out of your senior exec... Judith."

He almost spat out the name.

"Do you realise that her salary level is not a kick in the arse away from mine? And yet I've no idea what she contributes to the company. Take her salary out of the equation and you have an immediate, massive boost to the bottom line. And you never know, her departure might give you a bit more impetus to get stuck back into the private sector – a bit of oomph to add to that spring in your step."

That last remark stung Neville. It wasn't just an insult; it was a direct challenge to his authority. The bully was being bullied – and by a fellow-Ulsterman at that. But right now Jimbo was the star of the show, the company's saviour. This wasn't the time to argue with him. And, if truth be told, he hadn't been pulling his weight of late and really should be making more of an effort. As for Judith, well she was just collateral damage, wasn't she? He hadn't failed to notice the tension between Jimbo and her ever since the last office party. He had put that down to a lover's tiff. But perhaps there was more to it. Was Jimbo taking the opportunity to get rid of Judith after having been spurned by her? He would probably never know. What he did know was that there would be much shouting and tears from her and some sleepless nights for him before she was gone. He felt sick to the stomach.

"Gotcha! I hear you, Jimbo," he said, trying hard to look manly, as befitted the company boss. "Leave the business of Judith with me. She'll be out of here before you know it."

Jimbo picked up his copy of the draft accounts and rose to go. "That's brilliant, Neville. It'll all be worth it, so it will. No more chasing turnover to feed the staff, eh?

"Oh, by the way," he added when he reached the door, "there's a chap I used to work with at the SNHC in Edinburgh. He's leaving the place to set up his own consultancy. A bunch of SNHC managers from the west have organised a leaving do for him in Babbity Bowster's this Friday. I've been invited as well. He's coming through to Glasgow by train on Friday afternoon. So I thought I would meet him at Queen Street and bring him up here beforehand to see the office and meet you. He's called Dan McKay.

He's a Taig, but he's also a sharp guy who could be useful to us. He'll probably bring us some work through his consultancy."

Neville smiled and nodded. "No problem," he replied, but he hadn't been listening. He was still thinking about Judith. It wasn't that he cared for the woman or owed her any loyalty. It was simply that a confrontation with her was now imminent. And he detested confrontation. Added to that, his coffee had gone cold and dark, threatening clouds had amassed outside. Suddenly, life wasn't so good.

Chapter Four

Newcastle upon Tyne, 1990

When Neville and Jimbo turned the corner to be confronted by the lights and noise of Newcastle's Bigg Market, they both stopped abruptly with their mouths open.

"Holy fuck!" exclaimed Neville.

"Jeez-o," Jimbo said and whistled softly.

It was their first visit to Newcastle. After checking in at the Copthorne Hotel earlier that Friday evening, they had walked up from the Quayside to the city centre, stopping off at a restaurant in Dean Street for something to eat. They thought Dean Street was lively and friendly enough, but they were beginning to despair that Newcastle was another Leeds. They had gone to Leeds a couple of weeks earlier. "Leeds, the city that never sleeps" claimed the publicity, but they had spent a miserable, rainy Friday night tramping the streets in search of its non-existent nightlife.

The pair's brief visits to Leeds, York before that and now Newcastle were part of their quest to find a suitable location for the new company they wanted to set up in the north of England.

Back in Glasgow, Market Surveys Scotland was still doing well. Although the company's turnover had levelled out over the last year or so, the net profit had risen considerably thanks to the introduction of Jimbo's suggestions. Judith was long gone, albeit after a bit of a struggle. And the hike in prices had worked a treat, with only a couple of clients having been lost. Those losses had been more than made up by the extra clients brought in by Neville after he responded to Jimbo's taunt to "get stuck back into the private sector".

While there was no doubt that MSS was now a leaner and more profitable organisation, Jimbo had recently warned Neville against becoming complacent about its continued profitability. He predicted that the company's share of work in the public sector, particularly among local Councils, was unlikely to grow in the foreseeable future – and might even diminish. Scotland was a small country, he pointed out, with a finite number of potential public sector clients, all of whom were under sustained Government pressure to reduce their budgets. And when it came to expenditure cuts, spending on research was always a prime target. If profits were their goal, Jimbo argued, they would have to look to bigger markets outside of Scotland; in other words, the business would have to expand into England.

At the time of Jimbo's warning, both men were still riding high on the success of the company in Glasgow. They had had a taste of profits and wanted more – a lot more. To Neville, profits meant further property investment, just like his old Da had advised him. He had dreams of purchasing a holiday home in the UK, a pied-à-terre in the south of France and perhaps even a villa in Spain. For now at least, Jimbo had less expensive ambitions. To him, profits meant a bigger and better car, holidays abroad and that conservatory for his house. Most important of all, though, they meant money in the bank and the attendant security of a good bank balance.

Naturally, therefore, both were keen to set up operations in England. At the same time, however, recognising the need to be cautious not to overstretch themselves or their finances, they agreed that any expansion should be gradual and incremental. To begin with, they would establish a small regional office, a base from which they could promote themselves in the chosen region. They would employ minimal staff initially, perhaps only a PA, but might go on to hire a local manager if enough business was being generated. If, after a suitable period, the venture proved successful, turning a fair profit, they would move on to the next region, and so on until they had created a national network of offices. And if they ever reached that stage, they might have sufficient confidence and funds to go on to tackle the Holy Grail that was London, where the big boys hung out and where the big money could be made.

When they first discussed their plans for expansion, Neville had become so fired up by the concept of a network of regional offices that he began to talk of franchising the business.

"We could be like those coffee shops or those printing and copy places that are springing up everywhere. We supply the brand and the support infrastructure, they do the work and we reap the profits. We could be millionaires in no time, so we could!"

"Fuck's sake, Neville," Jimbo had snapped. "We haven't even set up the first office. And we don't know how hard or easy it'll be to get work in a market we know nothing about it. Catch a hold of yourself, will you?"

Ever since Jimbo's tirade in the boardroom in Glasgow the year before, that impatient, berating tone of his had been used with increasing frequency in his private conversations with his boss. Neville steadfastly ignored the tone; so long as Jimbo's disrespect stayed in private, he was prepared to put up with it. Anyway, as ever, he was desperate to avoid any kind of confrontation – not with the money-maker and definitely not at that time.

Having agreed that the initial regional office would become Jimbo's direct responsibility and should therefore be located within reasonable driving distance from his home in the east of Edinburgh, they had begun their search among cities on the eastern side of northern England. Several weeks and two disappointing city visits later, Newcastle suddenly seemed a promising prospect. Both men could feel a buzz about the place, an excitement they hadn't even remotely experienced in Leeds and York. Of the three cities, Newcastle was by far the closest to Edinburgh. And if what they were gawping at right now was anything to go by, the city had nightlife aplenty.

Loud voices and even louder music blared from the wide-open doors of the numerous bars that lined both sides of the narrow, winding street only yards ahead of them. Many of the customers of the packed bars had spilled out onto the pavement, bottles and glasses in hand, their strident conversations adding to the overall level of noise. The majority of the men outside were young, had close-cropped hair and wore tee-shirts. The women were also predominantly young with a uniformity of appearance: virtually all were blonde and, despite the mid-October temperature, wore little more than flimsy boob-tubes and micro-skirts, their bare midriffs exposed to the cold night air. This was Bigg Market in full Friday night swing.

The scantily clad girls held Neville and Jimbo fascinated. Neville drooled openly at the sight, but only Jimbo's dancing eyes betrayed his lust as they drank in the thighs and bellies and partially covered breasts on display. Notwithstanding their different outward expressions, the pair were thinking identical thoughts. Here they were: two well-heeled, smooth-talking, thirtysomething Irishmen, many miles from home and partners, with hotel rooms to go back to and the pick of any number of drunken, half-naked women to go back with.

"Fancy a beer or two?" Jimbo asked at last.

"Is the Pope a Catholic?" Neville responded.

As they walked towards the nearest bar, Neville decided that Newcastle was shaping up to be his most favourite English city. If all went well in the next few hours, it could turn out to be somewhere he might want to keep returning to. He could think of worse reasons for choosing it as an office location.

Chapter Five

Edinburgh, 1991

Dan tried to remain calm as he sat waiting for Jimbo to return with the drinks. Outwardly, he looked relaxed, almost laid back, but internally he was seething. He had already spent the best part of an hour waiting for Jimbo to turn up – and it had been a thoroughly uncomfortable wait at that. Ever since the SNHC moved to more modern offices down at Haymarket, the West End Wine Bar had become alien territory, frequented by strangers. And he had felt conspicuous in the midst of those strangers, nursing his pint and constantly checking his watch.

Because it was still early on a midweek night, the bar was less than half-full, but that only served to accentuate its shabbiness. It seemed to Dan that the old place looked more tired than ever, as if it had been used up and then discarded by SNHC staff. It had been a different matter two years ago when he held his leaving party there. That had been quite a night, a celebration of his twenty years with the SNHC. *The end of an era*, he had dubbed it. A good friend from the Computer Department who played fiddle in a folk band persuaded the band to come along. The Chinese restaurant across the road supplied a buffet. Best of all, he made it an invitation-only affair, giving him tremendous pleasure in *not* inviting colleagues who had wronged him in the past or whom he simply didn't like. Music, food and great company into the early hours. Yes, quite an event, though tonight it felt like such a long time ago.

His world had changed dramatically since then. He worked in the private sector now, running his own consultancy, his one-man band. He could have remained in a safe job at the SNHC, of course, with a good salary, eight weeks holiday and a protected pension, but a first meeting with his new line-manager persuaded him otherwise. Ian Smythe had joined the organisation's Administration Department a couple of years earlier, having recently retired from the Army with an officer's pension. From previous encounters with ex-Captain Smythe, Dan regarded him as an arrogant buffoon. This was the man who disdained to take part in inter-Departmental meetings and who instead sat and read the Financial Times, occasionally brushing imaginary fluff from his pinstripe suit, while those around him, including Dan, contributed earnestly to the company's business. This was the man who was often to be found in the corridors recounting tales of his last Army posting to Belfast, tales that invariably involved the men from his unit kicking down the doors of families on the Falls Road. And this was the man whom Jimbo's sham management consultants had decreed should be given a more senior role in the restructured company. Five minutes spent listening to his overbearing, public school voice at that initial meeting had been enough for Dan. He put on his coat, walked out of the meeting and headed straight to the Personnel Department to negotiate a redundancy package.

So, exactly twenty years to the day he began working there, Dan left the SNHC to start up his little consultancy. The redundancy payout was less than generous, but it tided him over for a few months, and he used some of it to purchase a word processor and a fax machine, together with a supply of business cards and letterheads. He also transformed his appearance, dispensing with the bearded Bohemian look to become a short-haired, clean-shaven, suited businessman.

Within a matter of weeks, the new company, called Housing Management Services Limited, was up and running, albeit from Alma's flat. Thanks in large part to a steady stream of commissions from newly appointed SNHC managers, who wanted the company to review their old systems or introduce new ones, the business had a very successful first year. And it had begun to receive commissions from housing organisations other than the SNHC. About halfway into its second year, however, the commissions began to dwindle, until now they were almost non-existent.

As far as Dan knew, all his clients had been more than happy with the outcome of the projects he had completed for them. He was certain, therefore, that lack of funding, rather than dissatisfaction with his consultancy, was the principal factor behind the work drying up. Although Thatcher was long gone, replaced by the less hard-line Major, the change at the top hadn't affected the Government's attitude towards public sector organisations, whose budgets were being squeezed tighter than ever.

Whatever its cause, the dearth of new commissions had placed Dan in the embarrassing position of having no income. He hadn't been in such a position since before he left school – and he didn't like it one bit. For the time being, he was living off Alma, who fortunately had recently taken up a job as Finance Manager of a local company, having graduated from university with an accountancy degree. While there was no pressure from Alma, who didn't seem to mind, he was pursuing every opportunity to secure new work. Which was why he was particularly keen to meet with Jimbo tonight.

He and Jimbo had been in regular contact during the last couple of years, but primarily for business rather than social reasons. That was because every other Housing Management Services project had required a survey of some kind or at least data processing and analysis services, work which Dan sub-contracted to Market Surveys Scotland through Jimbo. So much work was sub-contracted to MSS that Alma, who looked after the consultancy's accounts, couldn't help reminding Dan that the lion's share of his turnover each month vanished after paying their invoices.

"It's as if you're working for them, not yourself," she was at pains to point out, adding: "And nothing – no jobs, no leads – ever comes back from them. It's like a one-way street, Dan."

Dan couldn't argue with that, but he saw the relationship with MSS as a necessary evil, a way of enabling him to compete for projects that required more than pure consultancy work. He was also sure that Jimbo charged for the MSS work at less than the going rates, thereby helping Housing Management Services to be even more competitive. Always sceptical about anything that involved Jimbo, Alma doubted if the latter really was the case. As Dan discovered much later on, she was absolutely correct.

While Dan and Jimbo normally communicated by telephone and fax, they met up occasionally in Edinburgh, usually in the early evening, to discuss particular projects. Because it was located close to the gym that Jimbo attended and not too far from the SNHC's new offices, where Sally still worked, they continued to use the West End Wine Bar for their get-togethers. The last one had been about six months ago, although that turned out to be less of a business meeting and more of an opportunity for Jimbo to moan about his lack of success in finding work for the new company that he and Neville had set up in Newcastle. On a previous occasion, Jimbo had already regaled Dan with the tale of the pair's adventurous night in the city, leading to their decision to establish an office there as the base for the new company, which Neville apparently insisted should be called Market Surveys North-East. It seemed to Dan at the time that the choice of office location had been made with their dicks, rather than their heads. When Jimbo added that they had gone on to rent a small room in a serviced office block in Gosforth on the outskirts of Newcastle, only a minute's drive from the A1 and the route to Edinburgh, he had also wondered if they really were serious about expanding into England or if they were play-acting as successful businessmen. That latter thought was to occur to him many times again in the future.

At their last meeting, Jimbo related the sorry tale of his days in Newcastle attempting to drum up business.

"I drive down to that poky wee office in the morning," he had bleated, "and spend half the day on the phone to local Councils trying to squeeze out of thicko receptionists the names of the people who are responsible for commissioning research. It's like pulling teeth, so it is. But

I usually do get a name, even if it's only the Chief Executive. Then I spend the rest of the day stuffing brochures into envelopes, addressing them to the named contacts and dropping them into the postbox before starting the long drive home.

"Other days are worse. I spend the whole time on the phone trying to actually talk to the people who the brochures were sent to. To see if they received the material okay, if it's of any interest to them, if they'd like a meeting to discuss their research requirements – that sort of thing. But I rarely get to speak to the right people. And even when I do it's only for them to say that they'll keep us in mind for future projects – whenever that might be. It's a soul-destroying task, especially when you're doing it on your own. And I'm fucking sick of it, so I am."

Years before, during one of those rare occasions when Jimbo had opened up to him, Dan learned that his friend was an only child who had been brought up by his elderly mother, his father having died when he was just a youngster. So he hadn't been surprised when Jimbo began to act like a spoilt kid because things weren't going his way. At the same time, he had some sympathy for the man: in recent months, he had been carrying out precisely the same task to promote Housing Management Services – also without reward. What he said next to Jimbo had been a genuine offer of assistance, albeit one that might have turned into a piece of paid work for the consultancy.

"Listen, pal. I don't have much work on at the moment, so I'd be happy to come down to Newcastle for a few days to help you out. Finding contacts, stuffing envelopes, chasing up – I could do all that. For a fee, of course, although I'm sure it would be a reasonable one."

Jimbo had almost spluttered into his beer.

"You?" he laughed, incredulous. Then his look of incredulity turned into a sneer. "You couldn't do what I'm doing if your life depended on it. You're too lazy for that. You just don't have it in you after all those years wrapped up in your wee, safe, public sector cocoon. Sorry, Dan, but no thanks."

That response had stung Dan, especially since it came from the younger, more junior man he had gone out of his way to support for years in the SNHC. He felt like he had been kicked in the teeth. He was speechless and angry. When Jimbo suddenly finished his beer and left, saying it was time for him to go and meet Sally, he had become even angrier. He realised that he had been used by Jimbo, a bit of company for him while he waited for Sally to finish at work – it had been a Friday evening, after all. And he had vowed that he wouldn't let himself fall into that trap again. In fact, he had been so incensed that he would have been quite happy never to have spoken to Jimbo again.

Then, six months later, came a phone call out of the blue. It was Jimbo – the charming, affable Jimbo – looking for help. All his hard work chasing contacts had begun to pay off, he said. There had been a few bites, a few smallish jobs. But now he had received a brief for a major piece of research. It was from a large Metropolitan Council in the north of England. Potentially there was some big work in it for Dan. If he faxed a copy of the brief, could Dan have a look at it and perhaps come up with some ideas? Then maybe the two of them could meet up over a couple of beers to discuss their joint response to the brief.

Given his dire financial situation, Dan couldn't help but agree. Swallowing his pride, he read the brief and immediately became immersed in framing a response to it. Bradford City Council wanted researchers to evaluate a recent initiative of theirs called Community Government. Policy evaluation – it was right up his street and exactly the kind of thing he had wanted to do in the restructured SNHC. A major programme of public consultation was required, at the heart of which was a large quantitative survey of Council residents, bread-and-butter work for Jimbo and Market Surveys North-East. But there was much more to it than that. Interviews needed to be conducted with a whole raft of interested parties, including community and business representatives, local politicians and Council officers. Community forums across the Council area also needed to be consulted. And the results of all the different strands of consultation had to be brought together, conclusions drawn and recommendations made.

Dan could understand why Jimbo had sought his help in responding to the brief. He could also see plenty of scope for work for himself if MSNE was commissioned to carry out the research. So he had worked into the night typing up a draft proposal. And there he was the following evening with two copies of the draft, keen to discuss it with Jimbo, but desperately trying to keep his cool.

"Apologies once again, Dan," Jimbo said as he placed the beers on the table. Then, dispensing with his usual rigmarole of taking off and folding his jacket before beginning, he sat down, opened his briefcase and took out the original of the document he had faxed to Dan. "It's that drive back up from Newcastle," he continued. "It's a nightmare. Get stuck behind a slow-moving lorry or, worse, a farm vehicle, and a two-hour drive turns into three. They should ban those bastard tractors from the roads at peak times. A nightmare, so it is."

Dan didn't drive. Nor had he ever felt the need to learn. In his consultancy work over the past two years, he had travelled the length and breadth of Scotland using a combination of trains and buses and taxis. And he had done so without fuss, without complaint. He wanted to tell Jimbo: *Stop girning, for fuck's sake. Haven't you heard of "Let the train take the strain"? You could easily get the train from Edinburgh to Newcastle and back. And it only takes an hour and a half each way.* But he didn't. He simply nodded instead and lit a defiant cigarette.

In complete contrast to his normal over-reaction to cigarette smoke in his presence, Jimbo didn't even blink. *It's amazing what you'll put up with when you're after something, isn't it, pal?* thought Dan.

Jimbo resumed his monologue. "Aye, as I was saying on the phone, MSNE received its very first commission a few months back. From York City Council for a smallish community survey. There's a lovely girl there, a Research Officer in the Chief Executive's Department, who wasn't all that happy with the local agencies she'd been using and wanted to try out the new kid on the block. She's a satisfied customer so far, touch wood, so hopefully there'll be more work coming from that direction.

"And not long after the York commission, we were given a wee job – another community survey – by Bradford City Council's Chief Executive's Department. The Research Manager there is a bit of an anorak, a real stickler who knows his onions when it comes to surveys. But he's also a friendly wee guy whose policy it is to give new companies a chance. He didn't believe at first that we had any interviewers in his area, but now that we've completed the job to his satisfaction he seems to be a lot more confident about us."

Dan stifled a yawn. He felt like saying: *Why the fuck are you repeating everything you've already told me, Jimbo? You must like hearing the sound of your own voice. Get on with it, for fuck's sake!* But he stayed silent and continued to smoke, smiling politely at the appropriate times.

"Which brings me to this," said Jimbo, waving the document still in his hand. "He was certainly confident enough to include us in the invitation to tender for the big Community Government job. I know you've put together some thoughts on it, Dan, but maybe a bit of background before we discuss them?"

Smug cunt, thought Dan. "Sure thing," he replied.

Jimbo chuckled to himself, as if he was remembering a good joke. "I don't know if you know anything about the political situation in Bradford..."

Obviously not, smart arse.

"...but up until about a year ago the Council had a Tory-run administration. The Council Leader was a chap called Eric Pickles. Pickles being a very apt name, because, I'm told, he's a sort of Billy Bunter-type character. The man who ate all the pies, they call him down there."

Jimbo chuckled again, while Dan remained straight-faced.

"Anyway, Pickles had been trying to push through a load of Tory policies – reducing staff, privatising services, that sort of thing – and was not popular at all. Not surprisingly, the Tories were ousted in the local elections last year and Labour swept in. The new Council Leader is a young guy by the name of Tommy Flanagan. He's meant to be a pretty sharp character. This Community Government policy is his brainchild, apparently. He wants to see decisions taken by the community at grassroots level. To that end, he's set up about a dozen neighbourhood forums across Bradford. And eventually he wants each forum to have its own budget to spend on Council services as it sees fit. The policy was only introduced a few months ago, so it's still at an early stage. But before doing anything else, he wants to stop and take stock, find out what people think about the concept and how they feel it should be fine-tuned for the future. By people, he means everyone. The consultation is to be as all-inclusive as possible – businesses, voluntary organisations, community representatives, Council members and officers, as well as local residents. And obviously it will include a major survey of resident opinion."

He paused there to take a gulp of his beer. Dan reckoned that so far, other than the "man who ate all the pies" gossip, he hadn't learned much more than was already contained in the Council's brief.

"Now, about that residents' survey," Jimbo continued. "If we were commissioned to do the job, that's where we could come unstuck – big time. For a start, we would need to have in place a large field force of interviewers, and we only have a handful down there at the moment. And then, because Bradford has a high proportion of ethnic minority residents, mainly of Asian origin, the field force would need to include a good number of interviewers who are not only Asian, but also speak Urdu and Gujarati. Fuck, I can't even spell Gujarati! It would be a tall order, so it would, but Maisie... You've met Maisie, haven't you? Our Fieldwork Manager in Glasgow? I've a lot of confidence in our Maisie. She did an excellent job for us on those two wee surveys in York and Bradford. Anyway, just as soon as we receive word of the Community Government commission, Maisie has promised to go down to Bradford, get a major recruitment drive underway and stay there for the duration. That's the plan anyway."

Seemingly satisfied that he had imparted all he needed to, Jimbo took another gulp of his beer and sat back. Dan saw that as the cue for his contribution. From a folder he had carried with him into the bar, he pulled out the two copies of the draft proposal and handed one to Jimbo, saying, "You'll see I've had a go at writing proposals for the full research programme. The only bits I've left blank for you to complete are the details of the resident's survey – the sample size and structure and so on – and, of course, the pricing schedule. And obviously if we are successful in getting the job, we can then agree who does what within the programme."

Jimbo was sitting forward now, leafing through the pages, his mouth open. "Jeez, this is tremendous stuff, Dan," he enthused. "You've gone much further than I thought you would. Very impressive, sir. You know, with a proposal of this sort of quality, I think we could be in there with a big shout. If we can convince the Council that we have the skill-set and the resources to do the work, we could very well clinch it, so we could."

Long after they had both left the bar and gone their separate ways, Dan still felt uneasy about the meeting and its outcome. Naturally, he was pleased that Jimbo had appreciated his efforts. But at the same time he was severely disappointed because Jimbo hadn't considered that he had it in him to produce such a comprehensive document – even after their years working together at the SNHC. More than that, he didn't know if he actually liked Jimbo enough to work with him in what clearly would be a junior partner role. The alternative, of course, was to seek employment elsewhere and so lose altogether the autonomy he had enjoyed working for himself. No, he decided reluctantly, if he wanted to retain his independence, right now a partnership with Jimbo was the only game in town.

Chapter Six

Bradford, 1992

The Oak Inn in Bradford was one of those cheap, friendly, family-run hotels that are usually found on the fringes of city centres, their handful of rooms occupied on weekday nights by an assortment of sales reps, tradesmen and business people, all with limited expense accounts.

It was the hotel of choice for Maisie McCann during her frequent visits to Bradford. The Market Surveys Scotland Fieldwork Manager had practically camped in the place while she assembled and trained the interviewer team for the big Community Government job the year before. Her stays since then had been shorter but regular, required in each case because of yet another job having been commissioned by Bradford City Council. Neville had dubbed the Council "the dripping roast", a phrase Jimbo was fond of repeating at every opportunity in order to emphasise the success of the Market Surveys North-East venture – *his* personal venture.

The Oak Inn also served as a base for Jimbo and Dan whenever either or both of them came down to Bradford to conduct MSNE business and needed to stay overnight. It was joint business in connection with the latest Council job that had brought them there on this humid summer's evening. The job would require MSNE to conduct a programme of consultation to establish the community's priorities for the use of a vacant piece of land situated in the centre of the Manningham area of the city. To kick things off, they had been invited to say a few words about the forthcoming consultation at a public meeting in the area.

The purpose of the meeting had been to inform local residents about a number of initiatives that were planned in Manningham. While the MSNE project was included in those initiatives, the main focus of the discussions was on proposed measures to tackle prostitution and drug-dealing, both of which were endemic in the area.

The meeting was well-attended, with over a hundred people turning up. A couple of local Councillors and several Council officials were present. Representatives from the Police and the Health and Social Work authorities were also in attendance.

As expected, the MSNE project wasn't introduced until near the end of the meeting, so only about ten minutes were spent on it. Jimbo explained to the audience that residents would be consulted on three options for the use of the vacant land: it could be used to build much-needed social housing; it could be turned into a sports and recreation ground; or it could be the site of a purpose-built community centre.

If the initial reactions of people at the meeting were to be replicated across the whole of the area, it was evident that the community centre option would emerge as the most popular choice by far. That would have come as no big surprise to the Council. The large majority of Manningham residents were Asian, almost exclusively of Pakistani origin, a predominance that was reflected in the ethnicity of the audience. And for some time, representatives of the Pakistani community had been lobbying for the provision of their own centre. The outcome of the MSNE exercise may have been a foregone conclusion, therefore, but the Council wanted to be seen to have consulted everyone in the area, the scattering of White residents included, before committing resources to build the centre.

Although the MSNE "slot" had been brief and hurried, Jimbo and Dan were far from disappointed when they left the meeting to walk the few hundred yards back to the Oak Inn, which was located just outside Manningham. They had spent a highly entertaining hour and a half taking in the proceedings at the meeting, the highlights of which they joked about as they strolled, jacket-less, in the balmy night air that was heavy with the smells of spices and Asian cooking. Now, as they sat on stools at the hotel bar, drinking their first beers of the night, they continued to recount amusing incidents at the meeting.

"Jeez, I nearly ended myself when that bunch of prozzies came in at the back," Jimbo laughed. "And the big brasser, their so-called spokeswoman, demanding to know from the Peelers what was going to happen to their trade. Bizarre or what?"

"Aye, and those sleekit wee gets in leather jackets – their pimps, no doubt – slipping in at the back of them," added Dan. "Fuckin' bizarre, right enough."

Jimbo took a gulp of his beer and snorted when he remembered the next incident. "The best bit for me, though, was when that woman from the Social Work Department got up to speak. Telling everyone that the most effective way to tackle prostitution was to catch the young Asian men when they were still at school and teach them to respect women. Yeah, that's really going to deal with the problem quickly, isn't it? Makes you wonder what planet those Social Work people live on."

"Her talk certainly provoked a lot of laughter at the back of the meeting. And I did notice quite a few smirks on the faces of the Asian men."

"And not forgetting the Peeler Sergeant holding his head in his hands."

"Fuck, aye."

They both guffawed at the memory of that last image.

While Jimbo paid a visit to the gents, Dan ordered another round from George, the friendly, heavyset Yorkshireman who ran the Oak Inn with his wife. They would finish that round and then walk back into town to sample a Bradford curry for the first time. Over the months, there had been a lot of banter between Jimbo and George about which British city served the best curries. Jimbo, who considered himself an aficionado on the subject, argued that Glasgow won hands down, followed closely by Edinburgh. George challenged him to review his opinions after eating in “the Curry Capital of Britain”. And that was what Jimbo intended to do tonight. Dan would have preferred a Chinese or Italian meal, or even a plate of steak and chips, but he was happy to go along on Jimbo’s expedition.

In fact, Dan was quite happy with things generally. He was convinced that throwing his lot in with Jimbo to help MSNE win the Community Government project had been the right move. Since then, they had collaborated in tendering for, winning and undertaking a growing number of meaty projects across the north of England. In addition to the Manningham consultation exercise here in Bradford, “the dripping roast” that was the Council had just awarded them a three-year contract to monitor and evaluate the work of Bradford City Challenge, a company that had been formed to regenerate the run-down south-eastern area of the city using Government money from the City Challenge Fund, an urban regeneration initiative that was the brainchild of the Tory Environment Secretary, Michael “Tarzan” Heseltine. Moreover, the winning of that contract had automatically put them in a favourable position to bid for similar contracts from other City Challenge companies that were being set up in deprived urban areas throughout the country.

The employment situation for Dan now and into the foreseeable future was a very healthy one, therefore, but it wasn’t all plain sailing for him. There were certain aspects of his working relationship with Jimbo that he loathed. Not least of these was travelling as a passenger in Jimbo’s car, a prospect that would loom over him like a dark cloud the moment he woke up tomorrow morning. Jimbo was a Jekyll and Hyde character at the best of times. Sat behind the wheel of his car, he grew rapidly into an unbearable monster, whose wrath mounted with each perceived error or slight by other motorists and with each slower-moving vehicle that dared to impede the monster’s progress. Dan could only sit there tight-lipped, his nerves jangling, wishing the journey would be over soon, while the invariable upshot for Jimbo was that he would come to the end of the journey in the foulest of tempers.

Jimbo's motoring rages had even worsened in recent months since the acquisition of his so-called hands-free mobile phone. Despite weak and erratic phone signals, he would often use the device while driving in an attempt to conduct business within the company. Shouted, stilted, frustrating conversations with the Field or Data Processing staff in the Glasgow office or with his new PA in the Newcastle office were almost always cut off because of the signal disappearing. And then, of course, the folk at the other end of the line were labelled "morons" and "halfwits". Even Doris, Jimbo's polite and homely PA in Newcastle, was frequently called a "stupid cunt". Listening to these pointless pantomimes, Dan felt like screaming: *They can't fuckin' hear you, Jimbo. It's you who's the moron. Give it up, for fuck's sake, and give everyone a rest.* It seemed to him that the charades were yet another example of Jimbo trying to emulate a successful businessman and failing miserably.

Not surprisingly, Dan usually went out of his way to avoid sitting in the car with Jimbo, making excuses and sometimes lying barefaced whenever Jimbo suggested they should travel together. Even though he might have to leave the house earlier and arrive home later, or go down the night before if his appointment was for first thing in the morning, he much preferred to take the train. At least on the train he had space to read and think and perhaps do some work. And more often than not he would reach his destination relaxed and refreshed, rather than as a bag of nerves.

The journey down to Bradford earlier today had been a rare exception, as would the return journey tomorrow. With so much MSNE work going on or about to begin, there had been a need to catch up with Jimbo on a range of matters, which Dan had attempted to do in between Jimbo's abortive mobile phone calls and his frequent insults hurled at other drivers.

There were other things about working with Jimbo that Dan had come to loathe. He hated being introduced to Jimbo's clients with the words, *Have you met my father?* It was a joke, of course, to draw attention to the fact that he was smaller and older than Jimbo, but it was a joke that had worn thin very quickly. And he hated listening to Jimbo's cloying voice as he proceeded to butter up those same clients, many of whom happened to be young female Research Officers who appeared to be mesmerised by the sound of the soft Irish accent and the sight of the handsome beefcake. In fact, it had occurred to Dan early on that that attraction was more than likely a key factor in Jimbo's success in securing many lower-value jobs, the kind that Research Officers could commission direct without having to seek higher approval from their bosses. *If only they knew that the blarney was skin-deep*, Dan often thought. *If only they knew what lurked beneath.*

Because there were far more important matters at stake, Dan had learned to suppress his feelings about working with Jimbo, smiling politely at the jokes made at his expense, putting on his inscrutable face at other times. The key issue was that he was back earning good money. And the bonus was that he was carrying out work he enjoyed immensely: work that required him to use his brain to develop research frameworks, evaluate research findings and come up with practical recommendations; the very role he had been denied in the restructured SNHC.

There was also no doubt in his mind that by joining forces he and Jimbo had found a winning formula. Quality research proposals largely produced by Dan, coupled with Jimbo's confidence and charm in presenting them, had resulted in a string of successful bids, often in the face of competition from much bigger and more well-known research agencies. And with the recent Bradford City Challenge win, they now had a firm foothold in the field of urban regeneration, where the opportunities for research were certain to grow over the coming years.

Perhaps it was because he was buoyed by the latter thoughts of a steady stream of work well into the future or because he was already in high spirits after the public meeting in Manningham or because he was looking forward to a relaxing meal with an old friend, the first for a long time, or perhaps it was for a combination of all these reasons, but Dan made an uncharacteristically unguarded remark as soon as Jimbo returned from the gents and sat back down on his barstool.

"You know, pal," he blurted out, full of bonhomie, "that's some partnership we've got going. We're building success upon success. The future is most definitely looking bright for the two of us."

If Jimbo had had time to take a drink of his beer before Dan spoke, he probably would have choked on it. "Eh?" was all he could manage, his face taking on a panicked, horrified expression. All the work he had put in, all the worry he had put himself through, all those lonely hours spent in Newcastle scratching for jobs, all he had done to make MSNE a success, and this impudent wee Taig wanted to share the credit for it.

Then he recovered. "Let me be clear, Dan," he said coldly. "There's no fucking partnership, all right? As far as I'm concerned, you've been providing some support to *my* company on *my* jobs, on jobs that were won by *me*. *I* set up the company. *I* established the contacts. *I* developed the opportunities. You just tag along after all that. So don't be getting too far ahead of yourself, eh?"

Dan's bonhomie had disappeared, but he kept smiling. "You know something, Jimbo?" he spoke through his teeth. "Even if they had totally disagreed with me, most normal people would have nodded politely and moved on. But you're not normal, pal. There's something missing in you. I don't know if it's just you or if it's a general Belfast thing, but you lack the social graces, my friend."

Jimbo's response was to shove the barstool from under himself and storm out of the bar. From behind the counter, George watched him go before looking questioningly at Dan. Dan shrugged. "The big laddie's having a wee tantrum," he said and winked.

While George resumed washing glasses, Dan lit a cigarette and ruefully studied his beer glass. Jimbo had deserved a mouthful from him, of that he was certain. But he figured he had blown it all the same. He'd be back searching for work elsewhere soon enough. *Look on the bright side, though, McKay,* he chuckled to himself, *you'll be able to take the train home tomorrow – in perfect peace.*

Less than ten minutes later, George leaned over the counter, touched Dan's sleeve and indicated that he should look behind him. Bracing himself for a blow of some kind, Dan slipped down from his barstool and turned to confront Jimbo, who stood smiling with his hand outstretched.

"I'm sorry, Dan," he said, "but sometimes there's too much going on, too much pressure, and I don't stop to think. It goes without saying that I value your contribution to the company..."

"Maybe that's the problem, Jimbo. You never say it."

Jimbo lost his smile for a moment. He wasn't accustomed to making apologies, and he was finding this one very difficult. He took a deep breath.

"Well, I'm saying it now, Dan. The company wouldn't be where it is today without your input. And I'd really like that to continue."

Dan was still wary. He wondered if Jimbo was apologising because he realised he would be in deep shit if Dan walked away tonight. And he noted that Jimbo couldn't bring himself to repeat Dan's word: *partnership*. He was wary, but he was also pragmatic; his livelihood was what mattered here. He smiled back for the first time and shook Jimbo's hand.

"Let's go get that curry," Jimbo said with relief. "And enjoy ourselves for a change."

Dan winked again at a bemused George as the pair left the bar.

Chapter Seven

Edinburgh, 1993

When Dan walked into the New Town Hotel, he found that Neville and Jimbo had arrived there before him. They were sitting at a table in the lounge, deep in discussion. He was pleased to note that only a couple of other tables were occupied. The hotel, a converted townhouse, was one of a dozen or so dotted round the elegant Georgian and Victorian crescents of Edinburgh's West End. He had chosen this particular one for the meeting because he knew from his time working at the SNHC that the place was never normally busy during midweek lunchtimes.

Neville was the first to see him entering the lounge.

"Ah, it's yer man," he said, rising from the table and sticking out his hand. "Good day to you, Dan."

"Great to see you again, Neville," Dan replied, shaking the extended hand.

The big smile on Neville's face told Dan that the memory of their last bad-tempered encounter on the telephone several months before had been forgotten – or at least set aside for the meeting. The argument had been about the late payment of Dan's invoices. Fed up chasing Izzy for the payments and being fobbed off by her with excuses about severe cash flow problems, and then suddenly suspecting that his invoices were deliberately put to the bottom of the pile because he was regarded as a friend of Jimbo's and not a real creditor, he bypassed Jimbo, who probably wouldn't have helped anyway, and called Neville direct. The resultant conversation was so heated that both parties ended up slamming the phone down on each other. But the call had worked; the outstanding invoices were settled within a matter of days and subsequent invoices paid promptly.

"Can I get you something to drink?" asked Neville.

"Aye, thanks. A bottle of lager, please... Becks, if they have it."

As Neville went off to the bar, Dan shook hands with Jimbo and sat down at the table. Jimbo had a big smile on his face as well.

"I really appreciate you doing this, Dan," he said. "It'll be worth it, you'll see."

Before Dan could reply, Neville returned with a young waitress in tow. The waitress handed out lunch menus, took the order for Dan's beer and for another couple of bottles of water for Neville and Jimbo, both of whom were driving, and left to get the drinks.

When he had finished ogling her slim, departing figure, Neville waved his menu and declared, "As usual, guys, I'm staaarvin'. How about we order the food first and talk business later? Is that okay with you, Dan?"

"Sure thing," Dan nodded, trying to act nonchalant. He was eager to hear what Neville and Jimbo had to say to him, but he supposed he could wait a little while longer if he had to.

Jimbo had phoned first thing on Monday to say that he and Neville would like to sit down and talk with him about a matter of mutual benefit. The three of them could meet in Edinburgh at a time and venue of Dan's choosing. It wasn't hard for Dan to guess that they were going to offer him a job in the company. What he was keen to learn were the terms of the offer. He smiled and waited patiently.

With the main purpose of the meeting delayed for a bit, Jimbo took the opportunity to continue the conversation he and Neville had been having. "Just before you came in," he spoke to Dan, "Neville was telling me about the latest member of staff in Glasgow – the delightful Shelley. Yer man here has only gone and poached her from our auditors, so he has. Thinks she'll have a few tricks up her sleeve to help keep our tax bills down.

Isn't that right, Nev?"

Dan was very familiar with Jimbo's mocking tone, but he was surprised to hear it being directed at his boss. He thought it verged on disrespect. Neville didn't seem to mind, though.

"Aye, well," he laughed, "she's done us a few favours on the quiet during past audits, so she has. And I'm sure the auditors will forgive me eventually for taking her away from them. But seriously I needed to do something to lighten Izzy's workload. What with all the work you two guys have been pulling in and with Market Surveys Wales getting off the ground, not to mention the VAT man and the Inland Revenue hounding her, the poor girl has been run ragged. Izzy and Shelley will now divvy up the finance functions between them. And the best thing is that the two women get on like a house on fire, thus avoiding any potential catfights, which I fuckin' detest."

Dan observed the sneer that flitted across Jimbo's face at the mention of Market Surveys Wales. He had recently listened to a rant by Jimbo about what he called Neville's "lazy-arsed way" of setting up the new company in Cardiff. It seemed that Neville had stayed in that city for only a handful of days, during which time he succeeded in renting a small office near the city centre and in recruiting a manager to run the office. The manager was a feisty, thirtysomething, local woman called Sian, who had lots of market research experience, mostly for the private sector, and who was enticed to take the job by a handsome salary and the car of her choice, which turned out to be a nifty wee Lotus Elan. Jimbo had complained bitterly to Dan that, contrary to what had been agreed for the Newcastle operation, Neville had gone ahead and spent money on an office and staff in Cardiff without even a whiff of work coming in the door.

"Anyway," Neville continued, "bringing Shelley into the company should mean that we become much more efficient with things like chasing up client invoices and paying our cred–"

He stopped short, having suddenly remembered that angry exchange with Dan over unpaid invoices. The return of the waitress with their drinks saved him from having to finish the sentence.

When the waitress left again, this time with their lunch orders, Neville cleared his throat and began his spiel to Dan.

"Well, sir, I have to say that you and Jimbo have been doing a cracking job in the public sector, not just here in Scotland, but right across England as well. Fuckin' marvellous, so it is. I honestly don't know how yous do it. The work is so fuckin' demanding and so fuckin' complicated, I wouldn't know where to begin with it."

Having heard the latter statement for the umpteenth time, Jimbo gave a tired smile and stifled a yawn. Oblivious to Jimbo's antics, Neville continued.

"Obviously, therefore, the working arrangement you have with us is very valuable to the company. But it's also very loose – and I would say wasteful, with you having to agree prices with Jimbo for chunks of work and then invoicing us. And then, to our shame, having to chase us up for payment. So, as you might have guessed, what we're proposing today is to make the arrangement more permanent by inviting you to join the company as a Research Director.

"I'll go through the details of the position in a minute, but what I need to explain first is about the actual company you'd be joining. Now that we've begun to build up our network of companies in England, Scotland and Wales, I've recently set up a new company – a holding company – that'll be in overall control of the local companies. You'll not be surprised to learn that I've called it Market Surveys UK Limited. As I said, it'll overarch all the local companies, with the exception of Market Surveys Northern Ireland, which I'd prefer to ring-fence for the time being.

"Anyway, because you currently work on jobs for both Glasgow and Newcastle and in theory could work for any local office – there's no reason why you couldn't take on public sector work for Cardiff, for example – it's the holding company you'll be employed by. It's the same for Jimbo. And for me, of course, as Managing Director of MSUK.

"Now, about the post of Research Director itself. You'll have complete responsibility for bringing in and carrying out your own jobs from start to finish, for which you'll have full access to all the company's Admin, Field and DP resources, and for which we'll set you an annual turnover target. Jimbo has explained to me that you're still learning the ropes on the survey side of things, so we'll make sure the target is a very reasonable one to begin with. There'll be a salary, of course, which I'll come on to in a minute. On top of that, you'll receive annual dividend payments out of any profits that are made. Jimbo and I are trying to work out a way of formalising the profit-sharing arrangements, but in the meantime the amount of any dividends paid to you will be at Jimbo's discretion. We're also trying to figure out how we can extend share ownership to employees. Shares in MSUK aren't worth a bean at the moment, I know, but they will be in the future, mark my words. And we think people like yourself, people who contribute to the success of the company, should be rewarded with shares on an incremental basis."

Neville paused to take a drink of water. Preferring to wait until the full terms of the offer had been disclosed before responding or asking questions, Dan had simply nodded and smiled here and there while Neville spoke. He had met Neville several times before on visits to the Glasgow office, but only briefly on each occasion. This was the most he had heard him say at any one time. And he had to admit the man had the gift of the gab; *he could talk the hind legs off a donkey, so he could*, Jimbo had once told him. He had never found out from Jimbo what sort of work Neville did before market research, but watching him and listening to him today, he could swear he was experiencing a second-hand car salesman in action.

"The employee share scheme is something for the future, of course," Neville resumed, "but more immediately we need to talk about a starting salary for you. I know you don't drive, Dan, which is a pity, because the package I could offer you would be worth a lot more with the addition of a car. Without that, though, the best I can put on the table today is a salary of forty grand a year, which I think is more than you're earning at the moment and probably more than if you had stayed in your old job."

Knowing the source of the latter information, Dan shot Jimbo a glance, but Jimbo continued to study the glass in front of him without looking up.

"Now, you don't have to decide immediately," Neville spoke quickly, "although it would be preferable to know your initial reactions today while we're all together. If you do want the job, we'll draw up a formal contract of employment for you. It'll include things like your salary, the turnover target, holiday entitlements, and so on. And it probably goes without saying that you'll need to shut down your little consultancy company – either that or let it wither on the v–"

Jimbo, who had remained silent until now, suddenly chipped in before Neville could finish his sentence.

"A couple of things to add to what Neville has outlined, Dan," he said in that soft, deliberate way of his. "To begin with, there's the business of you working from home. That's been fine and dandy for your consultancy work, but if you do come on board with us we'll need you to become more *visible* in the offices, especially in Glasgow, where you'll have to be in pretty much constant contact with Field and DP."

"Izzy has already earmarked a room for you up in the attic," Neville interjected. "By the way, I've tried working from home a few times and failed miserably each time. I don't have the discipline for it. I just sit there, unshaven and still in my dressing gown, reading the paper or watching the telly. The last thing I want to do is any work."

"I'm exactly the same," said Jimbo. "I know from bitter experience it's just not productive," he added, looking directly at Dan, as if he was challenging Dan to disagree with him.

Dan didn't indicate whether he agreed or disagreed; he simply smiled and waited to hear what else Jimbo had to say.

"I don't mean you need to go into the office every day. Two or three days a week spent in Glasgow would be fine. And regular visits – say, once a fortnight – down to Newcastle. As you know, I'm currently looking for bigger office premises in Newcastle. Whatever we move into, I'll make sure there's a room set aside for you to use."

Since Jimbo's phone call on Monday, Dan had been mulling over how he might respond to the offer of a job. He had concluded that it all depended on the proposed level of salary. The level set out by Neville just now wasn't as high as he had wished for, but it *was* more than he was making from the consultancy – and considerably so. And there was the potential – no, the *likelihood* – of the salary being supplemented with dividends. There were other advantages, too. For a start, he would no longer have to rely on Jimbo's hand-outs. There would be no more chasing him round the country for information about particular jobs. If he was really lucky, he might not even have to collaborate with him on *any* jobs. Perhaps best of all, he would have total control over his own destiny within the company, in many ways retaining the autonomy he had enjoyed during the last few years. For all these reasons, he had been on the verge of accepting Neville's offer. But that was before Jimbo's interruption. That was before the man's overbearing tone had annoyed him.

What Jimbo said next wouldn't just annoy him; it would infuriate him.

"The other thing if you do take on the Research Director's job, Dan, is changing the *way* you work. I know that you type everything yourself. What you produce is obviously very neat and beautifully presented, but it must also be time-consuming – and your time will be too valuable for that. Typing is what the girls we employ do. I've been using a wee Dictaphone for years now. I dictate all my letters and proposals and reports that way. I often even dictate while I'm driving. Then it's just a case of chucking the tapes into Doris in Newcastle or the girls in Glasgow – they're all *audio-typists*, for fuck's sake – and Bob's your uncle. So my advice would be to nip into a newsagent's on your way home and buy a Dictaphone and a bunch of wee cassettes. You'll find a major difference when you begin to use it, so you will."

It took all of Dan's willpower to keep himself from exploding. *Take a deep breath and count to ten!* he screamed inwardly. *The cunt's deluded about that fuckin' Dictaphone of his, that's all. He doesn't know that his tapes are a standing joke among the girls, including his precious Doris, and the last thing they want to work on. They can't make out half of what he dictates because of that fuckin' accent of his. And they're all too afraid to tell him. The first transcript usually contains more asterisks for missing words than words themselves, for fuck's sake! And then the transcript has to go back and forth any number of times between him and them before they get it right. That's what you call fuckin' time-consuming, you big, sanctimonious arsehole!*

The smile on Dan's face had frozen into a rictus. He was so incensed that he couldn't find any words with which to answer Jimbo. But it didn't matter; the reappearance of the waitress carrying the first of their meals had diverted Jimbo's attention. "Lovely jubbly!" Dan heard Neville exclaim, and that image of a second-hand car salesman crept back into his head.

The further distractions created by the waitress bringing the two remaining meals, together with side-orders for Neville and Jimbo, allowed Dan time to calm down and consider Jimbo's stipulations. He thought the first one about spending more time in the offices, although expressed pompously, actually made good sense. The second one about using a Dictaphone he simply dismissed as arrant nonsense. He also concluded that neither of the stipulations altered Neville's original offer by one jot, so he decided to accept it there and then, quickly, before he changed his mind and before Jimbo could interfere again.

The two Ulstermen had already begun to eat when Dan declared, "I'll be very happy to accept that offer of employment, guys."

Two sets of knives and forks clattered down immediately.

Neville stuck out his hand. "Fuckin' brilliant, Dan," he mumbled, his mouth full. "Welcome to our wee family."

"Aye, welcome aboard, Dan," Jimbo smiled and offered his hand as well.

After he had shaken their hands, but before they could pick up their cutlery again, Dan added, "There's just one condition, though."

They both gaped at him.

"If I'm going to be pitching for and running my own surveys, I'll need to know the magic formula."

"Eh?" they asked in unison.

"The magic formula. The one that calculates the degree of sampling error for a known sample size."

"Oh, that," Jimbo grunted, remembering that Dan had been nagging at him for months to explain the formula. "I'll go through it with you next time we sit down together, I promise."

"While you're at it, Jimbo, could you could go through the formula with me as well?" quipped Neville. "I can't promise that I'll understand a word of it, mind you. Plucking figures out of the air is how I usually get by."

All three men laughed at the joke. With the business of Dan's employment out of the way, they could relax now, enjoy their lunch and talk of other things.

In between mouthfuls, Neville spoke excitedly to Dan. "Has Jimbo had the chance to tell you about my big news? About moving down to England?"

"Not yet," said Jimbo, while Dan looked blank.

"Yeah, well, last summer Izzy and I spent a couple of weeks in the south-west of England. Glorious countryside, so it is. And so much warmer than up here. At least ten degrees higher all year round."

"He's calling the weather down there continental," mocked Jimbo.

"Aye, well, and so it is. Certainly compared to Glasgow. Glasgow is just so fuckin' *cold* all the time.

"Anyway, we've decided to go and live in the south-west. We're looking at property in the Bristol area at the moment. There are some beautiful wee villages just a short drive from Bristol that we're interested in. And, of course, it goes without saying that Bristol will be the location of the next MSUK office. That'll be my next project once we move down – to set up Market Surveys South-West and get it running."

"Wow," was all that Dan could manage. There seemed to be a lot happening all at once.

"Yes, it's all happening," Neville continued, as if he had read Dan's mind. "And there's even more, so there is. With me planning to move away, I'm looking to find a replacement to run the Glasgow office and take care of the private sector work in Scotland. I've got someone lined up, a local chap called Jack Lamb. Jack's one of my clients, a senior partner at one of the ad agencies in Glasgow we do research for. He's been commissioning surveys for years. Now he fancies having a go from the other side of the fence, as it were. And it looks like he's very interested in taking the job."

"Aye, yer man Jack seems like a good guy," Jimbo added. "I met him in Glasgow on Monday when he came in to have a look round the offices. Definitely very keen."

"As I said, it's all happening, Dan," gushed Neville. "I'm confident the company is going to go from strength to strength in no time at all, so this is a great time to be joining it."

Then, without stopping to take a breath, he changed the subject entirely. "This driving business," he blurted out. "I'm really concerned about you having to rely on public transport to get anywhere. Trains, buses, taxis – it must all be a heck of a bind. I know you're a bit long in the tooth to begin learning to drive a conventional car, but what we could do is supply you with an automatic and throw in a few driving lessons. Automatics are so fuckin' easy; you just sit back and they virtually do the driving for you. That's how I got my old Da started, God rest him. After years and years refusing to even think about driving, he was scooting about in an automatic in a matter of weeks. So think about it, eh?"

By the time Neville had finished, Dan was seething again. *The pair of bastards were waiting to spring that one on me, weren't they?* he groaned to himself. *But don't blow it now, for fuck's sake, McKay. Just smile and agree. Then forget about it. They're not going to force you to drive.*

"I will, Neville, thanks," he said through his teeth.

Some fifteen minutes later, Jimbo and Dan were waiting outside the open main door of the hotel while Neville paid the bill at the small reception desk in the foyer. They could seem him gesticulating at the waitress and hear him arguing with her about the charge she proposed to levy on his credit card payment. The impasse was resolved when he declared that he would pay the service charge in lieu of the tip he had been going to leave her.

How fuckin' embarrassing, thought Dan. The second-hand car salesman was back in action.

The three men shook hands before going their separate ways, Neville and Jimbo to either end of the crescent to find their cars, Dan to the bus-stop at Haymarket for the short ride back to Alma's flat.

As soon as he turned the corner away from the crescent, Dan relaxed for the first time that day and lit a cigarette. He knew he should be feeling pleased with himself. All his hard work helping out Jimbo since that first job in Bradford, together with all the shit he had taken from him in the process, had finally paid off. He had come away with a permanent job worth forty plus grand a year; a job he actually liked into the bargain. He had retained what he could of his autonomy. And he hadn't committed himself to doing anything he didn't want to, like driving a car or using a fucking Dictaphone. Was it a case of lucky wee Dan McKay landing on his feet again? He *should* have felt pleased. But he didn't. A dark cloud seemed to be hanging over him, casting a shadow over his footsteps. It was as if he had just made a pact with not one but two devils.

Chapter Eight

Bristol, 1995

As was his custom when he first came into his office in the morning, Neville stood at the window, coffee mug in hand, and watched the comings and goings across the road in the large, tree-lined garden of Queen Square in Bristol. As was also inevitable each morning, his eyes were drawn to the centre of the garden and to the bronze, equestrian statue of William III that dominated it.

The presence of that statue was a stroke of luck that never failed to tickle Neville. Here he was, a true Ulsterman. And over there, only a stone's throw away, looking proud and mighty astride his war horse, was the very man to whom all true Ulstermen swore loyalty. King William of Orange. King Billy. The same King Billy who had knocked the shit out of the Papes at the River Boyne in 1690. How lucky was that, eh?

But it got even better. The building whose third floor Market Surveys South-West occupied – the building he was standing in now – was actually called King William House. You couldn't make it up! He loved having that name on the company's letterhead. And he delighted in telling people, especially the folk back home in the Province, that he had named the building himself.

When he decided on the office location, he didn't know about the statue or the building's official name, nor was he aware of Bristol's historical connection with King Billy. It was just one of a number of suites that were available for rent in the city centre. He chose it because of the magnificent setting of Queen Square and because it was only a short walk away from the string of lively bars and restaurants along the waterfront. Pure luck, so it was.

Sipping his coffee and continuing to people-watch, he tried to picture what the scene would have looked like back in the eighteenth century when the square was fashionable and all the buildings surrounding it were proper townhouses. There would have been horses and carriages trundling across the cobblestones on the road in front of him, of course. And over in the garden the gentry from the townhouses would have been swanning about in their finery.

He wondered for a moment if he and Izzy could rightly describe themselves as gentry – or at least the modern equivalent of gentry. They didn't live in a townhouse in the centre of the city – that wasn't fashionable nowadays – but they did own a large, newly-built house in a charming little village close to the airport and only a few miles from the city. The ground that came with the house was so big that it could easily accommodate a swimming pool, which he was seriously considering installing. Sometimes, when he went out walking the dog in the village, he actually felt like gentry, like a country squire. Especially if he was wearing his deerstalker and swinging his carved walking stick, both of which items he had bought at an antiques fair held in the village.

The statue of King Billy and the name of the building aside, Neville was feeling particularly lucky this morning. If he was a religious man, which he wasn't, he might even call it *blessed.* He loved everything about living in the south-west. He loved his house and the village. He loved the climate, which he still maintained was ten degrees higher than in Scotland. And he loved the people; they were so much more polite and softer spoken than in Glasgow – and in Belfast, God forbid.

He would even go so far as to say that moving down there had given both him and Izzy a new lease of life. He had a spring in his step again. And Izzy – well, Izzy had tidied herself up, hadn't she? With all the day-to-day finance work for the companies now being carried out by

Shelley in Glasgow, Izzy was a lady of leisure these
wife should be. She had much more time to look
house – and him, of course. Most evenings he could
steak on the table and a glass of cold beer. What mo
In fact, he was enjoying his new life with Izzy so mu
of making her an honest woman. And after marriage, who knew? Maybe children while he and Izzy were both still youngish. A couple of little Nevilles running about the house? Imagine that – him, Neville Brown, a family man, for fuck's sake. Who would have guessed it? But that was the influence of the south-west for you.

Mind you, being married didn't mean that he would have to go completely on the straight and narrow as far as other women were concerned. He still had the TA to fall back on for a bit of hanky-panky. Most of his TA buddies were married men, but that didn't stop them getting their ends off every other weekend. And he had a lot of TA weekends to look forward to, especially now that he was a Captain with a remit to make regular visits to all the regional training centres round the UK. Which was another thing that had happened since moving down. That and all the new business contacts he had made through the TA. A few of them had persuaded him to join the local Conservative Club, where he could mix with the "right" people. He was a successful businessman, after all, and the Conservatives were the Party for business. He liked the Club so much that he was even contemplating going into politics himself one day, perhaps standing for election as a town councillor.

But that was for the future. Right now, he needed to focus on the business itself, without which none of it – his TA career, his new life in England, even the daily presence of King Billy over there – would be possible. And, as it happened, the business was doing astonishingly well. Except for Bristol, which quite naturally was still at the early stages of development, all the offices were turning a profit. With the latest IRA ceasefire still holding, Belfast was experiencing a bit of a renaissance in the volume of work. Thanks to a lot of hard work by Sian, pain in the arse was, Cardiff was going like a bomb, pardon the pun. But the rs of the show were Jimbo in Newcastle and Jack in Glasgow. bo, with Dan's help, was continuing to win major public sector ontracts right across England and Scotland, while Jack had achieved a remarkable turnaround in the private sector side in Scotland, pulling in jobs left, right and centre from his former clients at the ad agency. Jack had also transformed the Glasgow office, bringing in a new executive team and making the place run far more efficiently than ever before. The guy had really got stuck in there, so he had.

Yes, Jack had proved to be an inspired choice for his replacement in Scotland. Another lucky find, just like Jimbo before that. Jimbo and Jack – the money-makers. It was just a pity they didn't get along with each other. But that, Neville regretted, was entirely down to him. It was one of those times when his luck deserted him. He had been so desperate to get Jack on board that he offered him twenty-five per cent of shares in Market Surveys UK Limited. And that was shortly after arranging for Jimbo's twenty per cent shareholding in Market Surveys Scotland to be converted into an equivalent shareholding in the new holding company. So he had made that offer to Jack in the full knowledge that Jimbo would end up with a lesser deal. What a twat he had been!

When he realised the trouble that the disparity would cause, he also realised there was nothing he could do to remedy the matter. He couldn't ask Jack to return any of his shares; that was never going to happen. Nor could he allocate an extra five per cent to Jimbo to even things up. If he did that, he would no longer be the majority shareholder and could easily lose control of the company, so that wasn't going to happen either. No, he had decided, he would just have to put up with the consequences of his mistake. Besides, he wanted to have a few shares available to allocate to others who were contributing to the success of the company – people like Dan. So long as he kept fifty-one per cent for himself: that was the cardinal rule in business.

The disparity couldn't stay hidden for long, of course. Jimbo discovered it when he received his copy of the first draft year-end accounts for MSUK. To say that he took umbrage would be the understatement of the century. He had been acting like a spoilt kid ever since; a spoilt kid who has been told he's no longer his mammy's favourite. His anger and resentment were directed at Neville initially, but when he saw that Neville wouldn't or couldn't budge, that nothing was going to change, Jack became his new target. Jack was Jimbo's enemy now, the usurper who had stolen his position as Neville's right-hand man. He was doing his utmost to outperform Jack, to discredit him and expose him as a charlatan. And Jack was rising to the challenge, quietly getting on with the job and becoming more successful by the minute.

Neville finished his coffee and with a sigh reluctantly turned away from his view of the square and King Billy in the centre of it. He knew the accepted wisdom about internal competition being good for a business. But he also knew that the type of competition begun by Jimbo might easily get out of hand and could end up splitting the organisation in two. As ever where Jimbo was concerned, though, he was powerless to do anything about it, other than to ride it out – and hope for the best, he supposed. And all because of a measly five per cent. He sighed again. The irony was that the shares weren't worth a fucking fig. They would only be of any value if he ever decided to sell the company. And that prospect was light years away.

He had barely returned to his desk and placed his empty coffee mug on it when the phone rang. He snatched up the receiver and spoke cheerfully into it.

"Meg or Charlotte?" he asked.

Meg and Charlotte were his two PA's. He had hired two because he wanted to make sure the office was covered at all times. Izzy had helped him recruit them, so they were a bit older, a bit more mature than the youngsters up in Glasgow. They were both lovely, bouncy, bright girls, though, who couldn't do enough for him. And he loved listening to their West Country accent; if he was being honest, that soft Somerset burr of theirs actually turned him on.

"Meg here," came the voice at the other end of the phone. "Sorry to bother you so soon, Neville, but I have Jimbo on the line looking for you. I said you might have already left to go to a meeting, but that I would check. Shall I put him through? He sounds... erm... keen."

Think of the devil and he'll be sure to turn up, Neville muttered to himself. Trust Jimbo to spoil an otherwise perfect morning. Yer man was always at it – scheming and plotting during the night and then phoning him first thing the next day. Unlike Jack, whom he heard hardly a peep from – that man just kept his head down and got on with the business.

"No problem, m'dear," Neville replied, still trying to sound cheerful. "Go ahead. I'll speak to him. Thanks, Meg."

He could do without it, but if he didn't take the call Jimbo would persist, phoning the office and his mobile until he got a result, so he might as well get it over with now.

When the call came through, he greeted Jimbo with as bright a voice as he could muster. "Good day to you, sir. What can I do for you on this fine morning? I'll be nipping off to see a client in a few minutes, but fire away meantime."

"A couple of things, Neville."

Neville shook his head. As usual these days, Jimbo had eschewed the common pleasantries. There was no *How are you, Neville?* There wasn't even a *Good morning*. Just those words. The guy was an arsehole.

"Sure, go ahead."

"Right. First of all, do you know that he's started signing himself as Managing Director of Market Surveys Scotland?"

"Who has?"

"Jack Lamb."

"Oh, Jack. Yes, that's right. He asked me and I said he could do that. He says that it'll sound more impressive when he pitches to clients. Why? Is there a problem?"

"No, no problem. I just wanted to know what was happening in

Glasgow, that's all. But if he's calling himself Managing Director, where does that place me in Scotland?"

"Look, Jimbo, it's just a title. You're perfectly free to use it as well for your clients in Scotland. I don't care what I call myself. But if people want to use fancy titles to help them win jobs, then that's fine by me."

Jimbo was silent for a while. When he spoke again, it wasn't to acknowledge Neville's last remarks, but to move on to his next point.

"We need to talk about putting down lines of demarcation."

"Uh-uh?"

"By all accounts, Jack's doing a tremendous job in the private sector in Scotland. But he needs to remember that his market is confined to the private sector. And it's a *big* market across the whole of Scotland. The public sector market in Scotland, *my* market, is much smaller, but it would be all too easy for Jack to encroach on it, especially when neither you nor I are in the Glasgow office very often nowadays. We – correction, *you* – need to remind him that that's not on."

"Sure, I can do that, Jimbo, no problem. As far as I'm aware, though, there hasn't been any such encroachment."

"That's just it, Neville. We're not aware. Which brings me to my next point. I'll set all this down in a memo and fax it to you later today so that you can look at it properly, but it seems to me that the organisation is running two distinct lines of business. There's the work that Dan and I do for the public sector, which I would term *social* research and which potentially we could carry out anywhere in England, Scotland and Wales. Then there are the more commercial types of jobs for the private sector that Jack does in Scotland, Sian does in Wales and you're now doing in the south-west of England. I think *market* research is the proper collective term for those latter jobs.

"So that gives us two discrete company divisions – the Social Research Division, which I head, and the Market Research Division, which obviously you take care of. I think if we formally introduce those terms into the organisation, it'll be a constant reminder to people like Jack and

Sian of the market they're supposed to be confining themselves to – a reminder of the lines of demarcation, like I said at the beginning. If you're happy to go ahead with that, I can start signing myself as Managing Director of the Social Research Division."

"On the surface, that proposal sounds perfectly logical, Jimbo," Neville gushed, happy to have been let off the hook so lightly. "I'll be away on TA business for a couple of days after today, but as soon as I'm back I'll look at your memo properly and touch base with you."

"Away playing soldiers again, eh?" asked Jimbo, unable to hide the sarcasm in his voice.

It was Neville's turn to stay silent, a tactic he had decided to adopt some time ago whenever Jimbo made a derogatory remark, his way of signifying that the remark was out of order.

"Anyway," Jimbo said eventually, "I do have another proposal for you to think about. It's a longer-term one following on from the creation of the two divisions. I'll put the details down in the same memo, but in essence it concerns the future arrangements for profit-sharing between the divisions."

Neville's heart sank. He wasn't being let off the hook at all. "Okay, I'll look at that, too," he replied weakly. "But right now I really do need to get off to that meeting."

Jimbo continued regardless. "I'm aware that MSUK is heading to show a sizeable net profit this financial year. I'm also aware that as a matter of course fifty per cent of the net profit will be ploughed back into the company reserves. It's what happens to the remaining fifty per cent that bothers me.

"So, roughly, here's what I'm thinking. With the aid of Shelley's new job accounting system, we'll know the profit that each job has made once the costs of Field and DP have been deducted from that job's fees. Which means that we can easily calculate the total job profits made by each division. From those figures, we then need to deduct each division's share of the company overheads, things like salaries and rents and so forth. But how should the overheads actually be shared? While it would be all too easy to go for a fifty/fifty split, that would ignore the fact that at the moment the Social Research Division consists of only three people – me, Dan and a PA – and operates out of a wee three-roomed office in Jesmond. The Market Research Division, by contrast, rents three offices, including that rather expensive one in Glasgow, and employs many more bodies. Apparently, Jack now has a virtual army of research executives, not to mention three – or is it four now? – Admin girls, none of whom Dan or I use any more.

"No, I think that something like an eighty/twenty split would be much more realistic. However, given that I do want to grow the Social Research team in the coming years, I'm willing to accept a seventy/thirty split today. But that would be it. It would be non-negotiable after that..."

"I'm sorry, Jimbo, but I have to stop you there. I need to go right now. And, to be honest, most of what you said latterly went right over my head. Go ahead and fax the memo. I promise I'll study it as soon as I can and get back to you."

Jimbo gave out an exasperated sigh. "Okay, bye," he said curtly. Then there was a click at his end of the line.

Neville replaced the receiver with a sigh of his own. He had understood perfectly what Jimbo was proposing. And he could see a lot of sense in the proposals. Aside from the problem of persuading Jack to agree to them, however, he feared they would simply hasten the scenario he had been dreading – the company being pulled apart.

He walked back to the window and his view of the square. He needed to handle all this carefully if he was to avoid that scenario. Perhaps he could draw some inspiration from King Billy over there. Or the Apprentice Boys who, against all the odds, successfully defended Derry's Walls for him. How did the words of the song go? *We'll fight and don't surrender*. Aye, that's it. That's what it'll be, Jimbo. No surrender!

Chapter Nine

Glasgow, 1996

The meetings had been Izzy's idea. In her capacity as Company Secretary of Market Surveys UK, she suggested to Neville that regular meetings of the three shareholders, with her and Shelley in attendance, might help Jimbo and Jack to become less mistrustful of each other and to begin working together in the best interests of the company as a whole. They would be an opportunity for Neville, Jimbo and Jack to be updated by Shelley on the latest financial position and to discuss future business prospects, any new business initiatives and strategic matters, such as the opening of new offices. Neville had run with the idea, decreeing that meetings of the Board should be held in Glasgow every quarter.

Proceedings were drawing to a close at the third such get-together. It, like the previous two, had been only partially successful. Shelley had disseminated the current turnover and job profit figures, which were very healthy, and each of the Directors had given their projections for turnover in the months ahead, figures that were equally healthy. But that was about it. Neither Jimbo nor Jack sought to divulge their plans for future business development; that was something they would do separately in private to Neville. And neither of them would succumb to enter into any form of discussion with the other. The hoped for thaw in the relationship between the two hadn't materialised so far; in fact, their relationship had grown noticeably icier as the series of meetings progressed.

Neville was well aware that the seating arrangement at the

meetings hadn't helped at all. On every occasion, Izzy, Shelley and Jack sat together on one side of the boardroom table, with Jack positioned nearest the corner, while Jimbo always chose to sit diagonally opposite Jack and therefore furthest away from him. Not wishing to imply that he was taking one side or the other, Neville always sat at the head of the table, which was his right in any event as chair of the meetings, but which meant that he and Jack were almost touching elbows. Inadvertent though it was, that proximity simply confirmed to Jimbo that Jack had become Neville's right-hand man.

Because the "Jimbo versus the rest" seating arrangement had been engineered by Jimbo, Neville felt powerless to do anything about it. Nor was he ever able, no matter how cheerful he tried to appear, to ease the tense atmosphere caused by Jimbo's permanent scowling face. While Jimbo scowled and the others did their best to ignore him, Neville fidgeted uneasily throughout the proceedings, frightened that at any moment an outburst from Jimbo might lead to some unpleasantness.

It was with much relief in his voice, therefore, that Neville closed the third quarterly MSUK Board meeting by saying, "Well, that's about it, folks, unless anyone has any other business to add."

But his relief was short-lived.

"Yes, I have something I'd like to discuss," said Jimbo, raising his arm to emphasise the point.

All eyes were on him as he swung his briefcase from the floor up to the table, clicked it open and took out a one-page document, which he proceeded to wave at Jack.

"I came across this page in one of *his* team's marketing brochures," he addressed Neville now, while pointing the document at Jack. "It's the page that lists his team's areas of expertise and previous clients."

He slid the document across the table to Neville and continued, "You'll see towards the bottom of the page a heading called *Health Promotion*, and below that a list of clients. A fair wee list of Health Boards in Scotland, so it is."

"Right?" asked Neville, clearly puzzled. He didn't understand what Jimbo's problem was. He turned to Jack for some enlightenment, but Jack kept his gaze fixed on Jimbo, an amused expression on his face, and waited to hear what more the latter had to say.

Still addressing Neville, Jimbo explained with an impatient sigh, "Health Boards are *public sector* organisations. I thought we made it clear many months ago that the public sector is the province of the Social Research Team, *my* team. We also had an agreement that any briefs coming into Glasgow from public sector organisations should be passed to me in the first instance."

With both Neville and Jimbo now looking at him, it was Jack's turn to respond. Like Jimbo, Jack was in his late thirties. He was also as tall as Jimbo, although much less powerfully built than him, an altogether more spare figure. Having dealt with aggressive Directors many times in his previous career in the advertising business, the Glaswegian wasn't particularly fazed by Jimbo's aggression. And he knew that meeting aggression with aggression was not the way to react. So he kept a smile on his face and spoke quietly.

"Two points, Jimbo. First, I've always been under the impression that when you talk about *the public sector*, it's a collective term for Councils and Housing Associations, who, as far as I'm aware, have formed your client base in Scotland up till now. I wasn't aware that there was any wider definition of the term."

"I have to say, Jimbo, that that's always been my understanding as well," chipped in Neville.

Jimbo shook his head and sighed. "When I say *the public sector*, I mean as opposed to *the private sector*. And Health Boards are certainly *not* in the private sector," he said slowly and deliberately.

"It's not rocket science, Neville," he added, hissing out the words.

After that interjection by Neville, Jack knew instinctively that what he said next would also be supported by his boss. He was delighted to see that the man was standing up to Jimbo at long last. So he went on more confidently this time.

"The second point is probably the more important one, Jimbo. It's about the *type* of work we've been doing for those Health Boards. In every case, we've been conducting surveys and focus group discussions to establish the effectiveness of the Board's health promotion material – things like leaflets and posters, but especially TV and radio adverts. That kind of stuff is my background, my expertise. And I don't think by any stretch of the imagination it could be described as *social research*. That's your term, by the way. You introduced it into the company."

"Jack has a very good point there," declared Neville on cue. "It's all to do with the type of research that's required, isn't it, rather than the sector? There's no reason, I suppose, why you couldn't carry out a social attitudes survey on behalf of a big private sector company."

Jimbo shook his head again. He was seething, not just because of Neville's backing for Jack, which came as no surprise, but mostly because of Jack's patronising and insulting tone. He vowed that he would never again put himself in a position where he would be subjected to that tone.

"Don't talk shite, Neville," he muttered. "This is the thin end of the wedge – and you know it. He'll be grabbing every brief that comes in the door soon enough."

Then he stood up, put on his jacket, slipped his papers from the meeting into his briefcase, closed the briefcase, picked it up and left the room, all without saying another word. He would not attend another MSUK Board meeting. Nor would he set foot again in MSUK's office in Glasgow.

When the door closed behind Jimbo, Jack shrugged, Shelley sat with her mouth open and Izzy glanced furtively at Neville. Neville returned her look. He wanted to scream at her: *This is all your fault, Izzy. These fucking meetings were your idea, you interfering bitch.* But he stayed silent.

Chapter Ten

Newcastle upon Tyne, 1997

Dan sat at his desk in the back room of the Market Surveys North-East office suite in the heart of Newcastle's Jesmond district. There were two other rooms in the suite: a bigger one adjoining his, which was used by Doris and her two assistants, and the largest one at the front of the building, which doubled as Jimbo's office and a formal meeting room, and which Jimbo could enter and leave without going near the Admin girls. The three rooms made up the ground floor of a two-storey house in an Edwardian terrace that had been converted over the years into offices for small businesses like MSNE, as well as into B&B's and doctors' and dentists' surgeries.

As far as Dan was concerned, his was a soulless room in a soulless office in a nondescript street at the arse-end of Newcastle – and he hated coming to it. There were no shops or cafés nearby where he could buy a sandwich or anything else. The nearest Metro stop seemed miles away, which meant that he had to take taxis there and back from Central Station in the city centre. And to make matters worse, he knew that the office location was highly convenient for Jimbo. The man could park his car in the space reserved for him at the rear of the building. As was the case with MSNE's first office in Gosforth, he could also reach the A1 and the road home to Edinburgh after just a few minutes' drive.

Naturally, Dan visited the place only when it was absolutely necessary, and even then for no more than a few hours each time. This morning was one of those necessary occasions, it being the day of the monthly meeting of the Social Research Team. The meetings had been held bi-monthly until recently, when Jimbo, in a fit of paranoia about the Team's performance, suddenly upped their frequency, declaring that he wanted "to keep a tighter rein on what people are up to". In addition to Dan, the original member of the Team, the "people" Jimbo had referred to were the two latest members, Geoff Longstaff and Hamish Rutherford, both of whom were in Dan's room at that moment. Like Dan, they were waiting for one of the girls to announce that Jimbo was ready to begin the meeting; he was, according to Doris, "on an important telephone call that might take some time". *We all have important telephone calls,* Dan had muttered to himself when he heard that, *but we still turn up on time for meetings.* He was sure both Geoff and Hamish would have had similar thoughts.

Geoff was standing at the only window in the room, peering out through its bars to the narrow back courtyard, where his car was parked directly behind Jimbo's. A sharply dressed, good-looking six-footer in his mid-thirties, he had been up since the crack of dawn to drive to Newcastle from his home in Aberdeen. He wasn't too pleased with the delay to the start of the meeting, but he was even less pleased with what he was seeing through the window.

"You know, lads," he said angrily without taking his eyes off Jimbo's car, "I've been arguing back and forward with Shelley for weeks now about getting another car. With all the mileage I've been clocking up recently, I really do need something newer and more powerful to get me up and down the motorways, specially since nearly all my journeys begin and end in Aberdeen. And you couldn't get further away than Aberdeen, min, now could you? But she's been claiming that money's tight and that no-one else in the company is being given new cars. And then this morning, after driving four shitty hours in the rain, I pull in here and discover, lo and behold, wor Jimbo has treated himself to a canny new car, a top-of-the-range Rover worth at least thirty grand, if I'm not mistaken. Aye, min, money's tight all right. My arse!"

Geoff was Newcastle born and bred. Even after ten years living in Scotland, his Geordie accent was as strong as the day he had moved up there. And it couldn't have contrasted more with the polished Southern tones of the next speaker.

"Yes, dear boy," drawled ex-public schoolboy Hamish, who was slouching in the chair behind the normally vacant desk opposite Dan's, "Jimbo told me about the car when he was on the phone the other day. Or should I say *bragged* about it. But I couldn't bear to go and see it when I arrived here today. And when I broached the subject of my own old banger needing replaced, he just told me to speak to Shelley. Which I did, but, as you'd expect, I received exactly the same brush-off from her as you have."

Hamish had flown up from Southampton airport that morning. He was also a six-footer, but there the similarity with Geoff ended. Portly, pushing fifty and casually dressed, he was an altogether more laidback character.

"Don't get me started about that girl Shelley," he continued. "She's the bane of my life at present. I have a running battle with her every month over my expenses. She seems to think I exaggerate my mileage claims. She's even gone so far as to accuse me of driving my wife and children over to France at the weekends and then claiming–"

"Which you would never do, of course," interrupted Dan. "Which you wouldn't even *think* about doing, isn't that the case, pal?"

"Certainly *not*, McKay!" Hamish exclaimed in mock surprise and then chortled. His laugh was so infectious that both Dan and Geoff joined in.

Hamish composed himself after some moments. "The point is," he said, wiping away tears from the corners of his eyes, "that lady behaves as if she has to pay the money out of her own pocket. She really does get totally on my tits."

"Mine, too," nodded Geoff, who by now had turned away from the window and the sight of the offending car.

"You guys just have to stand up to her," advised Dan. "Next time she queries your expenses, tell her to speak to Jimbo, and she'll soon clam up. She might be Neville's wee pet, but like everybody else she's shit-scared of Jimbo."

Dan was speaking from experience. During his four years as an employee of Market Surveys UK, he had had his own run-ins with Shelley about expenses. The problem began after he was about a year in. By that time, he had become aware of the full scale of the profit his jobs were making for the company and how insignificant his expenses were in comparison. By that time, too, he felt he had suffered enough personal inconvenience for the sake of keeping his job overheads to a minimum. At the end of a week of particularly horrendous train journeys and overnight hotel stays, he decided that henceforth he would go first-class on the train and he would only book himself into hotels that were at least four-star rated. There would be no more Friday night East Coast second-class train journeys in the company of drunken, rowdy squaddies returning to Scotland on leave from Catterick Barracks. And there would be no more uncomfortable nights spent in grotty, third-rate hotels that stank permanently of stale cooking smells. He would continue to make a buck for the company, but from that point onwards he would do so in comfort.

Naturally, Shelley complained bitterly every month about Dan's claims for first-class journeys and expensive hotel accommodation. Just as he had suggested to Hamish and Geoff, he invited her to take the matter up with Jimbo. The nagging soon stopped.

"I'm not surprised," Alma had remarked to Dan when he told her about Shelley's hostile attitude to his expense claims. "From what you've told me about her, she comes from an auditing background – and a junior level at that. Like most auditors at her level, she'll be more interested in saving the pennies at the expense of the pounds. She won't have any experience of management accounting. Worse still, I doubt very much that she's a qualified accountant. She seems to be nothing but a glorified bookkeeper. I couldn't think of anyone more dangerous being in charge of the accounts of a company your size."

In time, that last statement of Alma's would prove to be remarkably prophetic. But for now Dan was simply pleased that he could use his status as a star earner for the company to put the "glorified bookkeeper" in her place whenever it was necessary. He hadn't achieved that status easily, of course. In fact, when he received his contract of employment from Neville back in 1993, he had almost given up before starting. The "reasonable" annual turnover target promised by Neville turned out to be totally unreasonable, taking no account of the fact that he would be operating from a zero base, with no projects in hand and no regular clients. Added to that, the provisions for share ownership included in the contract were laughable. They stipulated that he would have to achieve or exceed the turnover target two years running before he qualified for a whole one per cent of shares in MSUK. And even then he would have to submit a claim for the shares *in writing* by a specified date, failing which his right to the shares would be forfeit.

Dan had been close to tears when he read the contract. He couldn't understand why Neville and Jimbo would deliberately compose such a mean-spirited document. It was as if they actually wanted him to fail from the outset.

Recognising his despair, Alma had been quick to offer her help. "You don't have to sign it, you know," she said. "We should be able to live off my money while you take your time to look for another job."

The tears really did flow then; no-one had ever been so generous to him in his whole life.

"Naw, you're okay, hen," he had replied eventually. "I'll sign the fucking thing. And I'll beat the bastards if it's the last thing I ever do. I'll make sure I meet their target and more. But I won't be writing to claim any shares – they can stick their measly one per cent right up their arses."

The first months were terrible for Dan. Jimbo tossed him briefs for research contracts that he didn't want to respond to himself – and that was the extent of his support. Every tender subsequently submitted by Dan was unsuccessful; either the pricing wasn't competitive enough or the proposed methodology wasn't right. With no turnover in sight, he resorted to working with Jimbo again on a handful of jobs. It was when they were returning by car from a meeting to do with of one of those jobs that he corralled Jimbo and urged him once more to write down and explain the formula for calculating sampling errors, which Jimbo did in between mouthfuls of his cheeseburger and chips at a Little Chef off the M6. There turned out to be two formulae, both of which Jimbo scribbled down on a page torn from his notepad. The page was still in Dan's possession today, folded neatly in two and tucked away safely in his wallet.

Armed with that vital information, Dan took some time to study a range of past tenders put together by Jimbo so that he could gain a better understanding of winning approaches and prices. The next tender he submitted was successful. And the one after that. And the one after that. The successes hadn't stopped since then. He now had a host of regular clients in England, spread across Yorkshire, the north-east, the north-west and the West Midlands, as well as a handful in Scotland. Their geographical distribution meant that he was a frequent InterCity rail passenger on both East Coast and West Coast lines and a frequent flier to Leeds-Bradford, Manchester and Birmingham airports. But he didn't mind the travelling or the stays away from home. He actually enjoyed his job. The expertise he had built up in the fields of housing research, urban regeneration evaluation and public consultation gave him a new confidence in the work he was doing. For the first time since leaving the SNHC some eight years ago, he was back at the top of his game again.

But, Dan had vowed, it was a game in which Jimbo would play as little part as possible. Not if he could help it. In the course of his examination of those previous tenders, he had made a couple of discoveries about the man which exposed him for the mercenary snake he really was and which obliterated any last vestiges of friendship that he may have still felt for him. Confirming Alma's suspicions back then, he found that the fees charged by Jimbo for the work sub-contracted by Dan's consultancy to

Market Surveys Scotland were *not* lower than the going rate; they were considerably higher. Even worse, he also found that the fees paid to the consultancy for work carried out by Dan on MSNE projects were a fraction – often as low as one-quarter – of the fees Jimbo charged his clients for those same pieces of work. The revelations made Dan more determined than ever to "beat the bastards". And he had proceeded to do just that. He was on course to exceed their turnover target for the fourth year running. He didn't claim his one per cent of shares at the end of the second year, but he did demand a sizeable salary increase, which Jimbo found hard to argue against. He was now receiving a salary of fifty grand a year, with annual dividends on top of that. His most recent dividend payment of ten grand seemed generous at the time, but now on reflection he suspected it was paltry in comparison with the amount of profit Jimbo had kept for himself.

The last four years had brought about major changes not only in Dan's working life, but also in his life at home with Alma. On the strength of his new job with its sizeable starting salary, he wasted no time in taking advantage of a dip in the housing market to secure a mortgage for a bigger and substantially better flat. The recently refurbished property occupied the basement level of a converted Georgian townhouse. It was spacious and airy, with a walled rear garden for his and Alma's exclusive use. And it was located slap-bang in the middle of Edinburgh's West End, just two minutes' walk from Haymarket Station on the one side and the same distance from Princes Street on the other.

Not long after furnishing the flat throughout and then moving in, Dan and Alma decided to get married. The wedding, a big family affair, had taken place a couple of years ago. While Dan happily included a few of his former SNHC colleagues as guests, he deliberately did not invite Jimbo and Neville and their partners.

On his first visit to the Glasgow office after the honeymoon, he discovered that his room there had fallen prey to the continued expansion of Jack Lamb's team – and, he suspected, the ongoing feud between Jimbo and Jack. Even though the room had been taken from him in his absence without so much as a by-your-leave, he didn't utter a word of complaint; he was glad to be rid of it. So now, when he wasn't out seeing his clients or pitching for new jobs or spending the occasional day in Newcastle, he worked happily from his new home, the spare bedroom having been kitted out as a proper office for him.

Although he still used his fax machine from time to time, the technology had moved on and he was now the proud possessor of a company laptop, together with a laser printer and an internet connection. The connection was a dial-up affair and not always reliable. Nevertheless, it enabled him to communicate both within the company and externally with his clients incredibly faster and easier than before. Neville, Jimbo and Jack had company laptops, too. When they first received theirs, both Neville and Jack had immediately enrolled in night classes to learn how to type. That made Dan smile. But he had to laugh out loud when Doris let it slip that Jimbo was continuing to send her tapes, on which he had dictated messages he wanted sent out by email, as well as his *replies* to emails from others. The digital revolution, it seemed, hadn't yet reached Mister Dictaphone.

Dan was also in possession of a mobile phone from the company. It was too big and heavy to carry in his pocket when he was out and about, so he kept it in his briefcase and switched it on only when he wanted to check for messages or make a call himself. There was a period a while back when he had used it regularly from home, going out into the garden to return calls from Jimbo and tell him that he was out seeing a client in Leeds or Liverpool or Manchester and therefore wouldn't be able to meet up with him for a drink and a chat that evening. He had had enough of Jimbo's little "chats" over a beer or two. They were always focused on the one subject: whether Jimbo should go ahead and recruit this person or that person as a Research Director in the Social Research Team. Every time they met, Jimbo dithered, asking Dan the same questions over and over again. Would they be up to the job? Was the market big enough to sustain them? The man was terrified of failure, but he felt compelled to do something because Jack Lamb in Glasgow was racing ahead in the turnover stakes.

The fact of the matter was that Dan couldn't have given a toss about what Jimbo did or didn't do. He wasn't there to support Jimbo. He was there to look after himself. It was *his* game, not Jimbo's. He grew so fed up wasting time on Jimbo's dilemmas that in the last of those calls from his garden he gave an exasperated sigh and blurted out,

"Look, pal, nothing's going to happen if you keep talking about it. You'll have to grasp the nettle sooner or later, so it might as well be now while the two guys are still interested. From what you've told me about them, they both seem capable enough. I would just go for it if I were you."

"Aye, I suppose you're right, Dan," Jimbo had muttered.

The conversation came to an end shortly afterwards, but Dan's outburst had done the trick. Jimbo proceeded to recruit Geoff first and then Hamish in quick succession. He had known both men for a number of years. Geoff was a client of his who worked at a senior level in the Housing Department of a Council in the north of Scotland. Hamish had spent most of his working life in the private sector, latterly as a senior consultant in a housing consultancy based in the south of England which regularly sub-contracted survey work to MSNE.

Dan could have predicted how the recruitment would be accomplished and what would happen afterwards. Jimbo would woo the guys. He would charm their wives. He and Sally would take them and their wives out to dinner. He would offer them attractive salaries and perks. He would bring them into the Glasgow office and introduce them to Maisie in Field and Trish in DP and Shelley in Finance. He would promise to set aside a room in Glasgow for Geoff and to rent some office space for Hamish, probably in Winchester where he lived. And then, when they had signed on the dotted line, he would leave them to fend for themselves.

Dan also knew instinctively that during the wooing process his own role in the company and the part he had played in getting MSNE off the ground would have been underplayed by Jimbo, if they were mentioned at all. Certainly at first neither Hamish nor Geoff had much to do with him. When they spoke to him, it was only in the passing and always with a sort of disdain, as if he was a member of the hired help. But slowly, gradually, as Jim's charm and approachability receded, they had sought his knowledge and advice, especially on sampling matters. Dan always found the time to respond to them, even to the extent of sharing the magic formulae he had spent years wresting from Jimbo. He liked to think that as a result the two men had developed more respect for him.

Their respect for Jimbo, on the other hand, seemed to be disappearing fast. His aloofness and general unwillingness to help, together with his curt and uncompromising attitude at their regular Team meetings, didn't endear him to them. Nor did the man's argumentative behaviour at their occasional social get-togethers. The last such event had taken place a few weeks before. Because Jimbo, Dan, Geoff and Hamish all happened to be staying in Edinburgh on the same night, they agreed to meet up for a meal at Jimbo's suggestion. That was the night when the new boys encountered the intolerant Jimbo for the first time. It was an innocent remark by Geoff that sparked him off. While the group waited to be handed menus at the restaurant, Geoff mentioned that he and his wife were planning to go to the cinema that weekend to see *Michael Collins*, Neil Jordan's recently released biopic of the Irish revolutionary leader.

"As an Englishman, I'm ashamed to say that I know very little about Ireland's history and England's role in it in particular," he said. "So I'm hoping the movie will help to fill that gap."

"Saw it a couple of weeks ago," Dan chipped in. "It's a good film. Not the most historically accurate, mind you, but it should give you a good understanding of the Easter Rising in 1916 and the War of Independence that followed. Oh, and Liam Neeson is brilliant as Michael Collins."

"Michael Collins?" Jimbo thundered. "What the fuck are you interested in him for? He was just a thug. A Fenian thug. A murderer." It was as if the Reverend Ian Paisley had suddenly descended upon them, spitting fire and brimstone.

The ensuing silence was broken when the menus arrived and Hamish asked, “Well, chaps, what’s it to be then? I quite fancy a Madras tonight.”

But even Hamish’s usually infectious humour couldn’t save the night after Jimbo’s outburst. Following an awkward and mostly silent meal, the group split up and went their separate ways. Geoff’s hotel and Dan’s flat lay in the same direction a short walk away, so the pair headed off together on foot.

“It’s like chalk and cheese, you know,” Geoff confided when they were close to his hotel. “Ever since I’ve known him, Jimbo has been as friendly as get out. You really couldn’t meet a nicer bloke. But the Jimbo I’m seeing now isn’t the same at all. I do get the fact that you can become a bit grumpy, particularly if you’re under a lot of pressure. But his behaviour tonight was totally out of order. Man, it was... well...”

Psychopathic, thought Dan.

“...frightening.”

“Obviously, you touched a raw nerve there just mentioning Michael Collins. In *his* mind, saying you were going to see the film was akin to saying you supported the IRA. But I agree, his reaction was totally over the top. And spoiled what otherwise might have been a pleasant night.”

Dan could have said a lot more, but he deliberately left it at that. He had no qualms about badmouthing Jimbo, but he needed to be sure of his audience; he didn’t want any of his remarks finding their way back to Jimbo.

And now, several weeks later, the gang was together again. Jimbo was still conducting that “important telephone call” from his spacious drawing room office, while Dan, Geoff and Hamish waited impatiently in the little back room. In readiness for the meeting beginning at a moment’s notice, the latter three were holding their copies of the Social Research Team’s monthly progress report. Compiled by Doris from information supplied by the individual members of the Team the day before, the report detailed the Team’s business activities during the previous month. There were lists headed *Tenders Submitted* and *Tenders Pending*, together with a third list simply called *Leads*. During the meeting, each member would be expected to report progress on the items bearing their name. They all knew, though, that the focus of Jimbo's attention would be on instances of tenders lost. The post-mortem he would proceed to hold in every such case usually consisted of a bad-tempered grilling of the unfortunate Director responsible for the failed tender. Invariably, therefore, the meetings were not a pleasant experience for anyone, Jimbo's chosen style of management being founded on fear and recrimination, rather than on encouragement and reward.

"Do we know what sort of mood our lord and master is in today?" asked Hamish. There were signs of strain in his usually relaxed and confident voice.

"Foul, apparently," Geoff replied.

"Fuck," Hamish swore under his breath.

"Aye," Geoff continued, "the girls were telling me that he hasn't come near them this morning. Just went straight into his office without even a *Good morning*. He does that a lot these days, they said. And he's been on the phone ever since – to Neville, they think."

"Fuck," repeated Hamish. "Just what I need. What *is* wrong with the boy these days?"

"I don't know," shrugged Geoff, " but, like I was saying to Dan the other night, he's not the chatty, pleasant guy I used to have a laugh with."

"Likewise, dear boy," said Hamish.

It seemed to Dan that the way the conversation was going he should no longer have qualms about badmouthing Jimbo in the presence of both Geoff and Hamish; he had found a pair of allies.

"It probably has a lot to do with this feud he's having with Jack Lamb," he declared. "He seems to be obsessed about the guy. And that's very likely why he's on the phone to Neville at this very minute."

"Aye," Geoff nodded, "Lamb can be a slimy bastard, right enough. I've been finding that out recently. Do you know that he told the girls in

Glasgow to tell me that I need to vacate my room there? I don't use it often enough, apparently, and it's needed for staff meetings. He didn't have the balls to tell me himself. And I've been loath to mention it to Jimbo – for obvious reasons. He'd go ballistic, min."

"He would that," agreed Dan. "And that temper of his seems to be getting worse. Alma happened to bump into Sally in Princes Street the other day. The lassie was almost in tears, apparently. She confided in Alma that often these days when Jimbo leaves the house he bangs the door behind him so hard the whole house shakes."

"Yikes!" exclaimed Hamish.

"He could have something mentally wrong with him, you know," Dan continued. "Just last night Alma and I watched a programme on the telly about how to identify psychopaths–"

"I saw that as well," said Geoff.

"Aye, well, out of the twenty characteristics of a psychopath they said to look out for, we reckoned something like a dozen applied to Jimbo. Things like superficial charm, self-importance, being manipulative, lack of empathy. Oh, aye, and pathological lying. I can't remember them all off the top of my head, but it was about a dozen."

Geoff stroked his chin and nodded to himself. "Like I said, I watched the same programme and didn't remotely think of Jimbo. But now that I come to think of it..."

"Yikes," repeated Hamish. "That is scary, chaps... if it is the case."

"Well, I don't know if it is," Dan shrugged, "but can I offer you guys a bit of advice before we sit down with the psycho... sorry, I mean Jimbo?"

Geoff and Hamish both laughed.

"Let's try and keep the meeting as upbeat as possible and not give him the opportunity to sound off. Don't volunteer anything about lost tenders. Just concentrate on the stuff you've won. There's the big Birmingham City Council job, in particular, Hamish, which you told me the other day had gone to MORI. You know, I know and the fucking world knows that the job was destined for MORI. Like all the big Councils, they want their survey to bear MORI's name. Like a hallmark. Unfortunately, oor Jimbo can't or won't grasp any of that. So my advice is not to tell him. Say instead that you're still trying to find out where the tender stands, but the Council are stonewalling–"

Before Dan could say anything else, Doris entered the room. She looked flustered.

"That's Jimbo ready now," she said, clearly out of breath, and held the door open.

As they left the room, Geoff gave Dan the thumbs-up sign, while Hamish smiled at him and whispered, "Good advice, McKay."

Dan followed them out. It seemed to him that the three of them were a little team now, united against a common enemy. It felt like the start of something.

Chapter Eleven

Costa Blanca, 1999

Jimbo sat at the edge of the pool with his feet trailing in the water and idly watched the ripples he was creating while he spoke into his mobile phone.

"Now, Maisie, I'm off to make myself a long, cold drink. Then it'll be another wee spot of sunbathing. But don't you be getting too cold and wet when you go out in the rain," he laughed, bringing his daily call to the Fieldwork Manager in Glasgow to an end.

"Aye, right, Jimbo," Maisie replied. She was thoroughly fed up by now with Jimbo's gloating. In all her years with the company, she had never known the Fieldwork Department to be so busy. Added to that, it *was* wet and miserable outside – again. And there was Jimbo not only lazing in the sun in Spain, but crowing about it at every opportunity.

"Lucky for some, eh?" she added sarcastically before hanging up.

Jimbo didn't notice Maisie's sarcasm. He was too busy feeling pleased with himself. One call to Maisie and one before that to Trish in DP to make sure his jobs were going well. Another call before those to Doris in Newcastle to check for any messages or post. And that was it – his workload for the day over. Now he could relax for the rest of the morning and the afternoon. In the evening, when it was cooler, he would stroll down to the village for a meal, a few glasses of the local *vino* and a bit of craic with the other customers. This was the life, so it was!

He stood up, took off his sunglasses, regarded for a moment the azure sky and the blazing, late morning sun in its centre, and decided that the long, cold drink could wait. He set down the sunglasses and his phone on the little plastic table at the side of the sun lounger nearest the pool. Then he stretched out on his back on the sun lounger. It was time to soak up some more rays. *No wonder things don't get done in a hurry over here,* he murmured to himself.

He closed his eyes and let the sun beat down on his finely toned, athletic body, already bronzed after almost a week spent at the villa. It was his and Neville's villa, jointly owned by them and rented out through a local agent when neither of them wanted to use it. And its location was ideal – up in the hills, away from the tourist-infested beaches, but only a short drive from Alicante airport.

Well, the place was his for the duration of the summer now, so Neville and Izzy could fucking whistle if they wanted some time here as well; they could go to their poky wee cottage in France instead. Besides, Sal would be taking a fortnight off her work and flying over at the weekend. Then it would be more like a holiday – for a while, at least.

Jimbo smiled to himself. He had been smiling a lot recently. He had stepped off the treadmill, no longer a part of the relentless quest for turnover that had been gnawing at his gut for such a long time. He was out of it now; away from the office politics and the poison that was Jack Lamb. He had escaped. And it had been so fucking easy. All it required was a bit of thinking outside the box and a quick word with Neville, who had almost fallen over himself to accept the deal.

And what a sweet deal it was. He operated his own little profit centre now. It was ring-fenced from the rest of the company's business. Fuck, *he* was ring-fenced from the rest of the company! He looked after a select group of clients, *his* long-established clients – folk like York City Council, who continued to commission jobs regularly. Half of whatever profit his jobs made was returned to the company. The other half was allocated to his profit centre. He didn't have to pay for anything else – no share of the company's overheads, nothing. And he could call upon the resources of Field and DP in Glasgow and of Doris and her girls in

Newcastle. On top of that, he was paid his full salary as usual and he kept his two company cars – the Audi for day-to-day business and the Merc for when he wanted to impress. All in all, he was actually doing better financially with the new arrangement – and for only a fraction of the effort and worry. Sweet wasn't the word for it!

And the Social Research Team? Well, it was Danny Boy's problem now, so it was. That was also part of the deal. Dan had been the natural choice to take over the reins. He had been behaving like the elder statesman of the Team anyway. Both Geoff and Hamish looked up to him, the girls in Newcastle loved him, and he couldn't put a foot wrong as far as Maisie and Trish and their staff were concerned. But Mister fucking Perfect had demanded his pound of flesh before he agreed to become the new Team leader. Aye, another hefty hike in his salary. Christ, the fecker was earning nearly as much as him now! By all accounts, though, he was doing a grand job – recruiting additional people to the Team, pulling in new work left, right and centre, and giving that gobshite Lamb a run for his money.

Dan's success in the job should have come as no surprise, he supposed. The wee man had been proved right about everything else. Especially the driving. After years spent by Neville and himself coaxing Dan to learn to drive, both of them were now converts to public transport, regularly forsaking the car for planes, trains and taxis. His own Damascus moment had come on a drive all the way from Edinburgh down to Redruth in Cornwall. Stupidly, he had tried to complete the journey as quickly as possible, without stopping properly. Well, in the end, he had been forced to stop for hours in a layby, having almost collapsed at the wheel. Jeez, he thought he was going to die that day! He found out later that a flight from Edinburgh to Bristol, another one from Bristol to Newquay and a taxi ride to Redruth would have taken him there inside three hours, arriving fresh as a daisy to boot. He was a convert after that.

And then there was the business of working from home. He had lost count of the number of times he had nipped at Dan to get his lazy arse down to Newcastle more often and work from there. How could clients have any faith in someone who sat about their house all day, unshaven and in their jeans and tee-shirt? That was his argument, anyway. But, in the event, it didn't matter a fuck to them, did it? Not so long as their jobs were completed on time. Look at the bold Jimbo now with his laptop and his internet connection, working – if you could call it that – from the poolside of a Spanish villa. Home-working was becoming more and more common these days. The world was changing – and Dan could see that change coming years ago. The same with the typing. Even he had succumbed to doing his own; it was still a two-finger job, mind you, but it did the business. No-one used Dictaphones any more. And no doubt Dan foresaw that as well. Aye, Mister fucking Perfect, all right.

Of course, under his new role, Dan would now have to have regular dealings with both Lamb and Neville. The devious and the spineless. Well, good fucking luck to him. As for himself, he had just one last matter to sort out with Neville before he stepped away from that relationship as well. It was to do with the shares he owned in MSUK. The way things stood at the moment, the shares would be returned to the company if, God forbid, he were to be run over by a bus tomorrow. And that wasn't right. He had worked his butt off for those shares, so it was only fair that they should be passed on to his surviving partner. In that way, Sal would reap the benefit if the company ever was sold. Or she could sell the shares back to the company. Either way, she would get something back for all his efforts. As far as he was concerned, it was a simple enough matter for the lawyers to sort out, but you'd think it was a major operation the way Neville spoke about it. The last couple of phone calls he had made to Neville about it had become rather heated, to say the least. For some reason, yer man was acting tough after all these years as a wimp. Maybe Jack Lamb was objecting to the change, goading him on. Who knew? But he would get it sorted out sooner or later. It was the only cloud on the horizon of an otherwise perfect world.

A trickle of sweat running into one of Jimbo's ears prompted him to turn over onto his stomach. Letting his arms dangle at either side of the sun lounger, he put the dispute with Neville out of his mind for the time being and thought of more pleasant things. Once the summer was over and he was back in Edinburgh, he would make a point of spending more time at his cottage in the Borders. It was a lovely wee retreat in a village at the foot of the Eildon Hills. Like the villa here, he had been encouraged by Neville to buy it. Neville was a great believer in property investment; "insurance against the future", he called it. Whatever, he'd also make a point of going to the cottage on his motorbike, his Matchless. He had kept that old bike running for twenty-five years now, ever since he bought her in Belfast when he was a teenager. He loved spending hours on her down in the Borders, whizzing round the B roads, which were almost always deserted. What a tremendous feeling it was: just him and the old girl eating up the miles, the trees and hedges and telegraph poles flashing by. Exhilarating, so it was!

With images of him on a silver Matchless flying through the countryside, Jimbo dozed off. While he slumbered, more clouds began to form on his near-perfect horizon. Over in Glasgow, an incensed Maisie complained to Shelley, the first person she bumped into after her conversation with Jimbo. Shelley delighted in immediately passing the details of Maisie's complaint to Jack Lamb. And Jack Lamb lifted his phone receiver and hit the speed-dial button for the Bristol office. Neville needed to know that no-one was happy with Jimbo's behaviour.

Chapter Twelve

Newcastle upon Tyne, 2001

It was two o'clock on Friday morning when the bar at the Vermont Hotel on Newcastle's Dean Street was finally closed. The only customers by that time were the Market Surveys people from across the road, who had been out on the town celebrating and who had booked ten of the hotel's rooms for the night. The three locally-based admin staff took taxis home. While some of the other celebrants, including a "rather whacked" Hamish, headed for their rooms, the remnants followed Geoff to his room, where he had offered to raid the minibar and supply them with a nightcap. Geoff was usually careful with the pennies and his favours, but it was a case of hang the expense on this occasion. Besides, the company was paying for everything; Dan had made sure of that.

Like all the "executive suites" at the Vermont, Geoff's room was quite spacious; certainly spacious enough for his six guests to make themselves comfortable while he busied himself at the minibar. Dan and Jimbo made beelines for the only two seats and sat across the room from each other. Gavin plunked himself down on the windowsill. Maisie and Trish perched politely at the foot of the double-bed, but Helga, with a Marlene Dietrich-like gesture, stretched full-length on it, her head propped up by several pillows.

With Geoff's back to him and with a mischievous smile on his face, Dan called over to Gavin, "Will you do me a favour, pal, and open that window so that I can have a wee puff?"

"Aye, McKay," Geoff said without turning round to look at Dan, "you just try lighting up in here and your cigarette will gang oot that window with you ganging reet after it."

Dan laughed out loud. He had no intention of smoking in Geoff's room; the threat to do so was a bit of devilment on his part to wind up Geoff. He had had a good night and a lot to drink, and he was still in the mood to party. But it wasn't the alcohol alone that kept him feeling merry; it was also his continued delight with the incredible success he and his people – the Social Research Team – had achieved. That success was the reason for their celebrations into the small hours.

During the financial year recently ended, the Market Surveys UK group of companies collectively had exceeded the one million pound turnover mark for the very first time, with the Social Research Division having been responsible for bringing in some two-thirds of that figure. According to Shelley's calculations, after taking account of its job costs and its share of the company's overheads, the Division was expected to have made a net profit for the year amounting to a cool two hundred thousand pounds. And half of that sum would be retained by the Division, to be distributed by Dan between himself and the members of his team in accordance with a formula he had already agreed with each of them.

As if a hundred grand's worth of dividends wasn't sufficient cause for celebration, there was also the present financial year's position to consider. The Division had made a storming start to the year and was already projecting a higher annual turnover level than in the previous twelve months. The reason for its continued success could be summed up in two words – *Best Value.* While the policies introduced by successive new Governments often required some form of public consultation, thus spawning work for the market research industry, the Blair Government had gone one better. Not only had they invented the buzzword Best Value, they had also made it a statutory obligation for local Councils to ensure Best Value in the provision of their services by consulting with their service users on a regular basis. Since the consultations were to take the form of quantitative surveys, this meant that every Department of every Council in the land needed to commission a market research agency to conduct the surveys on its behalf. Of course, many of the larger Councils went straight to the big, well-known agencies, prepared to pay a premium for their surveys. But many other Councils sought more reasonable prices from the likes of the Market Surveys UK companies. As a result, MSUK was currently immersed in conducting Best Value surveys across England, Scotland and Wales – and would continue to be into the foreseeable future.

While the fortunes of Dan and his team were soaring, the opposite was the case for their Market Research Division counterparts in MSUK. The Bristol office still hadn't turned a profit, the Cardiff office was just about managing to break even and the executive team in Glasgow, despite being regularly increased by Jack Lamb, was struggling to win new work. Overall, the Market Research Division was projected to record a massive net loss for the previous financial year. And prospects for the Division in the present year weren't looking promising either. All of which amounted to yet another cause for celebration by the Social Research Team.

Dan had arranged for the night out in Newcastle to be preceded by a "special" team meeting. He had also invited Neville, Jimbo, Maisie and Trish to come to both the meeting and the night out. Maisie and Trish were delighted to be invited and readily agreed to make the trip down from Glasgow. Surprisingly, Jimbo also agreed to come out of his self-exile. Not surprisingly, Neville declined the invitation, making the excuse that he would be away on TA business. Dan knew that was a lie. As far as he was concerned, Neville didn't want to offend Jack Lamb by overtly supporting the Social Research Team and celebrating what Jack saw as its "unfair" success: unfair, he complained, because his team bore the lion's share of the company's overheads, while the Social Research Team contributed a paltry thirty per cent. With the two teams now roughly the same size, he argued that the seventy/thirty split agreed between Neville and Jimbo years earlier should become a fifty/fifty split. Having calculated that even with a fifty/fifty split the Market Research Division still wouldn't have turned a profit, Dan had concluded that arithmetic wasn't one of Jack's strongpoints. But it didn't matter anyway, because Neville would not be moved on the matter; it seemed that he would far rather put up with Jack's wheedling than with the combined wrath of Jimbo and Dan.

When he took over as Head of the Social Research Division a couple of years earlier, Dan had attempted initially to develop a closer working relationship with Jack. But it had been a one-way effort on his part. Although Jack was always pleasant in their conversations, he was also patronising, putting himself across as an expert in his field, some kind of market research guru. And it was clear that he disdained the work of the Social Research Division. While Jack's superior attitude was irritating at worst to Dan and his team, a recent development had really put their backs up. On behalf of Market Surveys Scotland, Jack had accepted an award from the local enterprise agency in Glasgow for *Fastest Growing Business, Small to Medium Size Category, 2001*. Obviously, this was good news for the company, but what incensed Jack's Social Research colleagues – and Jimbo, of course – was the content of his application for the award. The way it read, Jack had singlehandedly turned a third-rate Glasgow-based market research agency into a UK-wide operation with a million pound turnover. There was no mention of the parts played by Neville, Jimbo and Dan; it was only he who was credited with such an amazing turnaround. And this despite the fact that neither he nor any members of his team had ever undertaken any projects outside Scotland. It came as no surprise to those assembled, therefore, that Dan closed his celebratory team meeting with the words, "Keep up the good work, people. And let's mess some more with Jack Lamb's head."

For their post-meeting party, the team had taken over the upper floor of a popular restaurant in Newcastle's Chinatown. They had also hired a mobile karaoke machine, together with a DJ to operate it. So there had been plenty of good food and drink and music and singing until the restaurant closed. Then it was down to the Vermont to continue the party in the hotel bar.

The Vermont was the usual venue for the team's social get-togethers. It was located only a few yards from the Market Surveys North-East office in Dean Street in the heart of Newcastle. The office, which comprised two large adjoining rooms in a beautifully restored Victorian bank building, was a five-minute walk from Central Station. It had been handpicked by Dan when the lease for the previous premises in Jesmond came up for renewal. The move to the new office coincided with the departure from the company of Doris and both of her assistants; oddly, all three had gone off on maternity leave at more or less the same time. The latter departures meant that Dan was able to begin afresh in new premises with his own admin staff – three young, keen people who were very loyal to him. Needless to say, his trips down to Newcastle were now much more frequent.

The two most recent additions to Dan's executive team were also young and keen. Both were in their mid-twenties and both were very able Research Directors. There was Gavin, who used to work in the research department of a large Council in Scotland which was a regular client of Geoff's. Then there was Helga, who came over from Germany to study in Southampton and stayed. She was originally recruited by Hamish as his PA, but was soon running her own projects.

While Geoff passed out the drinks to his guests, Dan sat with a big grin on his face and listened to the banter between Gavin and Helga, Gavin holding forth in his broad Lowland Scots tongue and Helga, smart as a whip, retorting with that very pronounced, crisp German accent of hers. Then Dan caught sight of Geoff handing Jimbo a bottle of beer and his grin disappeared. *Jimbo!* He had been so quiet that Dan had forgotten all about him. But there he was, seated in the middle of Gavin and Helga's friendly crossfire – and looking decidedly unhappy.

In the weeks preceding the meeting and night out, Dan frequently asked himself why he had invited Jimbo to come along. It wasn't out of friendship or loyalty, he was sure of that. Nor was it because Jimbo was actively involved in the company's work; on the contrary, commissions from Jimbo's "ring-fenced" clients had all but dried up in recent months, leaving him with little to do except collect his large salary every month, a situation which was known to many in the company and which rankled some. No, Dan decided, it was more than likely that he had included Jimbo out of plain bonhomie, out of a desire for everyone to share in the Social Research Team's success.

Whatever his reason for issuing the invitation, Dan regretted it immediately afterwards. He regretted it more when Jimbo accepted. He worried about how Jimbo would conduct himself. Would he hijack the proceedings and attempt to dominate them? Would his presence create tension during what should be a happy occasion? In the event, Jimbo behaved perfectly. He was respectfully quiet, almost subdued, throughout the meeting, nodding and smiling at all the right times. He became more animated and more chatty after a few drinks at the restaurant, even participating in the karaoke singing at one point. And at the Vermont bar afterwards he was just one of the merry crowd.

But the expression now on Jimbo's face told a different story. Eyes narrowed, jaw set, mouth tight – Dan had seen that dark look many times before. It was the precursor to an explosion of temper. Dan's booze-addled brain recognised the danger, but was too slow to do anything about it. Then Helga inadvertently pulled the trigger for the explosion.

Her conversation with Gavin having been interrupted by the arrival of drinks from Geoff, Helga turned her attention to the quiet man on her right whom she hadn't met before yesterday's meeting.

"Well, Jimbo, I understand you are a man of leisure these days. Tell me, what is it you do to fill in your time?"

The question was asked softly and languidly, but Helga's German accent made it sound like the beginning of an interrogation.

"You cheeky wee hussy," Jimbo snapped. "Why don't you mind your own fucking business?"

"C'moan, Jimbo," a concerned Gavin began, "Helga was only tryin' tae be friend–"

"I was speaking to her," Jimbo snarled at Gavin. "So you fucking butt out of it."

Dan could hear his brain screaming at him. *Wake up, for fuck's sake! The big fucker is bullying your staff. People you care for. You should be protecting them. You should be doing something.* And at last Dan reacted.

"Jimbo!" he yelled across the room. "That's enough!"

An unrepentant Jimbo glared back at him, but said nothing. The whole room fell silent. Then Maisie broke the silence by declaring, "Well, folks, I think it's time for ma bed."

"And mine," agreed Trish.

Geoff sighed. "Aye, I would say the party is well and truly over, people," he said glumly.

Without another word being spoken, all of Geoff's guests trooped out of the room. Trish, Gavin and Helga went left to go to their rooms on the same floor. With their rooms located on higher floors, Maisie, Jimbo and Dan went in the opposite direction, heading for the lifts at the end of the corridor. It was when the three of them had stepped into an empty lift that Dan couldn't hold back any longer. He was angry. Angry with the squalid way in which his team's glorious celebrations had been brought to such an abrupt end. Angry with the interloper whom he had invited into the fold and who had abused his hospitality.

"What the fuck is wrong with you, man?" he growled at Jimbo just as the lift began to ascend.

Jimbo responded immediately. It was as if he had been biding his time for Dan's rebuke. "I'll show you what's wrong with me," he hissed through clenched teeth.

Then his right fist came swinging at Dan's face. His own anger, fuelled by the resentment that had been building up in him all day and all night, was blind to the fact that wee Maisie stood between him and Dan. The blow went over Maisie's head and would have knocked Dan senseless had the latter not blocked it with his left forearm, thereby lessening its impact to a mere graze on his cheekbone.

Now, Jimbo may have been a six-foot muscle-bound rugby player who trained regularly at the gym, but he was not a fighter. And Dan may have been six inches smaller and many stones lighter, but he did know how to fight. As a skinny runt at a large, rough school, he had learned how to take care of himself, to stand up to the bullies and thugs who roamed the playground. With the help of a surly, but benevolent, PE teacher, he had also learned the rudiments of boxing.

"Hit fast. Hit often. Hit from the pit of your stomach. And hit where it'll hurt most," was the PE teacher's advice, which Dan was now following to the letter – and not for the first time since leaving school.

Still blocking Jimbo's right-hand, Dan used his own right to fire a rapid volley of punches into Jimbo's face. While the big man reeled backwards, Maisie winced and ducked with each punch. Then the lift stopped, the doors slid open and she flew out and along the corridor.

Being unable to counter Dan's barrage of punches with any punches of his own, Jimbo now resorted to using his superior strength to stop the assault. He grabbed Dan's left wrist and held it in an iron-like grip. Then he caught hold of Dan's right fist, prised the fingers open and slowly bent them back. Dan was now powerless to move, and the pain going through his hand was excruciating. He knew that his fingers could snap at any moment, so he took the only sensible way out of his predicament and suddenly went completely limp.

"What the fuck are we doing here, Jimbo?" he asked calmly.

The strategy worked. Jimbo immediately let go of Dan and stood back, panting. As if they had agreed telepathically to do so, the two men then stepped out of the still open lift together and sat down on the ground opposite it, their backs to the wall of the deserted corridor.

"What the fuck was all that about, eh?" Dan continued. "Two grown men behaving like idiots." There were adrenalin-induced tears streaming down his cheeks as he spoke.

With the beginnings of tears also forming in his eyes, Jimbo simply nodded in response.

They sat there for a while, catching their breath, saying nothing, giving their emotions time to settle down. Finally, Jimbo reached out and patted Dan on the shoulder. There was a smile on his face; it was the smile of Jimbo, the charmer.

“Come on,” he said, “let’s go and find Maisie. We need to apologise to the poor woman. We must have nearly scared her to death.”

As Dan pulled himself up and dusted off his suit, he thought to himself, *The man really is a fucking psychopath!*

Chapter Thirteen

Glasgow, 2002

When Dan stepped down from the first-class compartment of the Edinburgh-Glasgow shuttle train and onto the platform at Queen Street Station, he was still unsure of the purpose of that morning's meeting. Neville had been very vague in his phone call the previous evening, as if he, too, was unsure. All Dan knew for certain was that Neville and Jack wanted a discussion with him about Jimbo's future in the company. And they wanted the discussion to take place away from the office at a venue of Dan's choosing. So Dan had chosen the lounge of the Copthorne Hotel, which sat in George Square right next to the station and which he often used on his journeys to and from Glasgow.

He crossed the concourse, exited the station by its main door and took a few steps to his left to stand outside the Copthorne's side entrance, where he lit a cigarette. Then, for perhaps the twentieth time since Neville's call, he went through in his head the events leading up to the meeting.

Apart from a phone call on the day after their fight in the lift of the Vermont, he hadn't heard from Jimbo during the intervening months. That call, which came as soon as he arrived home from Newcastle, had been oddly conspiratorial, with Jimbo behaving like he and Dan were two bad boys who had been up to some mischief. He seemed to be more concerned about how the incident had affected Maisie, rather than how Dan felt. And, of course, there hadn't been a word of apology from him.

Dan smiled as he recalled the morning after the fight. There were a few scratches down the side of his face, his right hand ached, and he had a bit of a hangover, but otherwise he was fine. Once he checked out of the hotel, he crossed the road and went up to the office, where he discovered that all the other revellers had checked out before him. Most had already left for their various destinations, but a small delegation, consisting of Hamish, Gavin and Helga, had hung back to speak to him. Hamish was their spokesman.

"We feel your pain, dear boy," he said. "Maisie told us what occurred. She said you were getting the better of the big bully when she scooted off. We just wanted you to know that if you're dismissed because of it, we'll walk out with you. And that goes for all the other members of the Team. We can set up another company. We'll be much better off on our own, away from those bastards."

The prospect of being fired for defending himself against an attack by Jimbo hadn't occurred to Dan. It was a possibility, he supposed, but he dismissed it lightly.

"I'm sure it'll no' come to that, Hamish. But thank you. Thank you, guys. Your support is really, really appreciated." And he genuinely meant that.

Dan was proved correct: other than in that one call from Jimbo, the fight wasn't mentioned again by anyone, although he was certain it was common knowledge throughout the company. He thought it highly likely that both Neville and Jack knew about the incident. Jack, who frowned upon drinking in general and staff nights out in particular, would have put it down to drunken shenanigans by the Social Research Team. The man seemed to have a Presbyterian outlook on life; *Work hard and don't enjoy yourself* was his motto.

While there had been no further contact from Jimbo since the fight, Dan had received plenty of phone calls from Neville. The calls were usually in the evening and often at the most awkward times, but each time Dan had responded politely and tried to be helpful. Invariably, the calls had concerned Jimbo's behaviour during his long-running communication with Neville over the future ownership of his shares in the event of his death. It seemed that every time Neville sent him a fresh draft of a legal agreement, Jimbo rejected it and demanded more, often in the most abusive terms.

At first, Neville tried to find out from Dan what had gotten into Jimbo, why he had turned so nasty and angry. Dan had no qualms about suggesting that Jimbo could be mentally unstable, that he was exhibiting all the characteristics of a psychopath. Then Neville sought Dan's advice on the best way to handle Jimbo. Dan's counsel was always the same – hang up if Jimbo becomes abusive on the phone and don't respond to insulting emails from him; in other words, don't give in to the bully.

Even though he often regarded them as "nuisance" calls, in which he found himself saying the same things from one call to the next, Dan was pleased to have been contacted by Neville. By confiding in him and seeking his help, Neville had treated him as an equal, not as an adjunct to Jimbo, for the first time in his nearly ten years with the company. The beginnings of a rapport had developed between them. Whether Neville actually acted on any of his advice, Dan didn't know. What he did know was that Neville was becoming increasingly frustrated with and worried – even frightened – by Jimbo's behaviour. Perhaps it had all come to a head. And perhaps that was the reason for the meeting today. He would find out soon enough.

Dan finished his cigarette, pulled back the glass door and entered the hotel. The lounge was only a few steps away on his right. As he approached it, he could see that, as expected, Neville and Jack were there already, occupying a table in the corner. When he reached the table, Neville stood up immediately with a big grin across his face.

"It's yer man, Dan," he said, shaking Dan's hand vigorously. "What can I get you to drink? A coffee? Tea?"

"A cappuccino would be nice, thanks, Neville."

While Neville walked over to the bar to speak to the waiter, Dan sat down across from Jack, who had remained seated, smiling his false smile.

By the time they shook hands and exchanged pleasantries, Neville had returned to the table.

"Thanks again for coming along at such short notice, Dan," he began. "We really needed to get away from the office. Too many big ears there. And I'm glad you picked this place. I like it. Very handy."

"Yeah, I come in here any time I need to wait for a train back to Edinburgh. Much better than sitting in the station."

"Right. Well, you'll not be surprised to learn that this meeting is about Jimbo. More precisely, about Jimbo's exit from the company. I've now reached the end of my tether with him, so I have. The last phone call from him yesterday was nothing but a string of invective. He has to go. And he knows it. The question is how."

Neville paused there while the waiter set down Dan's cappuccino.

"Yes, the question of how," he resumed when the waiter had gone. "Jack was all in favour of simply firing him–"

"And still is," interrupted Jack.

"Fuck, Jack, I owe Jimbo more than that. For all the years he put into the company before he turned into... a monster. Besides, I can't let him walk away owning twenty per cent of the company's shares. I have to get him to agree to return the shares. I need to do a deal with him."

Jack was still smiling, but Dan was sure he could hear him sighing.

Neville cleared his throat and turned his attention back to Dan.

"Before I go into the details of the deal, though, I... well, we... need to hear from you, Dan. You're a major player in the company now, but you're also Jimbo's friend. You've known him even longer than I have. Because he goes, we wouldn't want to lose–"

"Let me stop you there, Neville," said Dan, putting a hand up. "I *was* Jimbo's friend at one point. But not any longer. Over the years, he's bullied me, belittled me, insulted me, cheated me out of money and even physically attacked me. I don't owe him anything. I don't have the slightest vestige of loyalty left for him. I'd like to get rid of him as well. And the sooner, the better."

"Fuckin' hell, Dan!" exclaimed Neville, shaking Dan's hand again. "It's good to have you on board, sir."

Dan noticed there was a genuine smile on Jack's face now.

"But I still have to hear about the deal," he added, smiling as well.

"Alright then, here's what I'm proposing. Thanks to both you guys and your Teams, we're a company that's rich in reserves. What I'd like to do is use some of those reserves to buy back Jimbo's shares. But to space out the payments to him over a number of years so that we don't hurt the company and don't really feel the pain. And bear in mind that while the reserves will go down annually, we'll more than make up for it elsewhere by losing Jimbo's big salary and all his other expenses."

"So what sort of money are you talking about... to buy the shares, that is?" asked Dan.

"I have in mind an upper limit of three hundred thousand. But I'll start the negotiations at two hundred. We'll probably agree on a figure somewhere between those two sums."

"Wow!" was all Dan could say, while Jack sighed audibly this time.

"But remember what we're trying to achieve here, guys," Neville continued. "The primary objective is to get shot of Jimbo and retrieve his shares. Thereafter, the secondary objective is to effect a reallocation of the company's shares. We need to bring you into the fold for a start, Dan. And there are others in the company who should also be rewarded with some shares. Shelley, for example."

Dan furrowed his brows at the mention of Shelley's name, but that word *reallocation* had him very interested.

"Well, if we're talking about reallocating shares, I'll have some of *his*," he said half-jokingly while nodding in Jack's direction.

Jack's smile vanished immediately. His whole being tensed. "Over my dead body," he growled.

Well, well, well, thought Dan, *Mister Bonhomie Lamb's mask has slipped at last. The wolf has bared its teeth.*

That reaction of Jack's was something Dan would never forget. But it was his turn now to smile falsely at Jack.

Neville tried to make light of Jack's response.

"Sorry, Dan, I should have been clearer. Jack's shares aren't up for grabs. Nor are mine. What we're talking about is reallocating the shares we buy back from Jimbo. That's twenty per cent we have to play with. I'm thinking of allocating five to Shelley and the rest to you. By the way, by rights you should already have a couple of per cent under your belt, but you don't appear to have bothered applying for them."

That last remark annoyed Dan. But something big for him was about to happen, which he didn't want to mar by explaining to Neville exactly why he hadn't fucking *bothered* to apply in writing for the shares. Instead, he simply grinned and shrugged. Then he said:

"Okay, then. But if you're going to give shares to Shelley, you have to do the same for Maisie and Trish. Those two are as important, if not more important, to the company as Shelley. And the allocation has to be significant, not merely token."

Neville seemed puzzled. "But the more I give to others, the less there'll be left for you."

"Understood, Neville. But right now, both Maisie and Trish are much more important to me than a few shares. So how about this? Three per cent each to the three ladies and the balance of eleven per cent to me?"

Neville still looked puzzled. "I'm fine with that, I suppose. But what about you, Jack? What are your thoughts?"

Jack had his false smile back. "I think what Dan's proposing makes good sense, Neville. I'm happy with it as well."

Dan felt Jack's reply was so insincere he might as well have added: *It's no skin off my nose, really, just so long as my twenty-five per cent remains intact.*

"Great!" declared Neville, rubbing his hands together. "And over and above the fifty-one, which I must hold on to for obvious reasons, I'll have a few per cent to hand out to our star Research Directors – people like Geoff and Hamish, perhaps."

Dan could swear he heard Jack sighing again.

"But first of all I need to speak to Jimbo," Neville continued in a less confident voice. "And that won't be an easy task, I can tell you..."

Less than half-an-hour later, as he returned across the station concourse to catch his train home, Dan couldn't help grinning at the outcome of the meeting, which he had already begun to refer to as *The Copthorne Agreement.* With Jimbo certain to go – he surely couldn't resist an offer of that magnitude of money – only three key players would be left on the field. And he was one of them. He would be a significant shareholder to boot. And he would have achieved something for both Maisie and Trish. It had been a good meeting.

Chapter Fourteen

Glasgow, 2003

The inaugural meeting of the reconstituted Board of Market Surveys UK was meant to be a celebration of the rebirth of the company, but with the news of Jimbo's tragic death in Morocco still fresh in their minds none of those present were in the mood to celebrate. The six shareholders were there, the duo of Neville and Jack having now been augmented by Dan, Maisie, Trish and Shelley. A heavily pregnant Izzy was also in attendance as Company Secretary. All were seated in the boardroom of MSUK's new headquarters in Glasgow's Southside.

The location of the office, in the heart of the grimy streets of Shawlands, was a far cry from the Victorian splendour of the Park district. But, with the old office having become too small for the company's ever-expanding staff, bigger, less expensive premises needed to be found, a task which Jack had accomplished with relish. The new premises occupied the spacious ground floor of a modern four-storey office block and were open-plan for the most part, a feature which most of the staff disliked, but which more than suited an increasingly autocratic Jack. The office came with a large underground carpark, so there was no more squabbling among the staff over parking spaces. It was also much closer to Jack's home, a fact that he didn't let on to Neville when he persuaded the latter to agree to the lease.

Maisie and Trish were taking part in their very first Board meeting, and were nervous as a result. By contrast, Shelley, who had attended many past Board meetings in her capacity as Finance Manager, seemed perfectly at ease. And Dan? Well, this formal meeting came after at least a dozen informal discussions between him, Neville and Jack since The Copthorne Agreement over a year ago; it was the culmination of all his efforts at those discussions.

Neville opened the proceedings in a sombre tone. He was still reeling from Jimbo's death, still harbouring some guilt over what appeared to him to have been a suicidal stunt by Jimbo.

"Thanks for coming along, people. But for the recent tragic event in Morocco, today would have been a happier day for all of us. I don't think we'll ever learn what compelled Jimbo to go out alone into the middle of the desert and ride his motorbike without a crash helmet. Whatever the cause, it was such a waste of a life."

Everyone shook their heads in unison.

"Such a waste," repeated Jack with what Dan suspected was mock-sincerity.

"As you'll probably know," Neville continued, "the funeral was held in Belfast at the weekend. Izzy and I sent flowers to Sally. And Jack also sent her flowers on behalf of the company."

Flowers from fucking Jack! thought Dan. He wondered how Sally had reacted to those; she was bound to have known that Jimbo hated the man with a passion.

"Yes, our hearts go out to the poor girl, so they do," said Izzy.

"Which is why I've told her that the company will honour its debt to Jimbo," Neville added quickly. "For those of you who don't know, we did a deal with Jimbo when he left the company. We agreed to buy back his shareholding for the sum of two hundred and forty thousand pounds, which we also agreed to pay in three equal annual instalments..."

At the sound of that amount, there was a sharp intake of breath from Maisie, while Trish could only stare with her mouth open.

Neville smiled. "Well, it was the only way we could get hold of the shares and redistribute them. But don't worry, the payments come out of our reserves, so they're not really felt by the company. Shortly before his... em... unfortunate accident, we had paid over two instalments to Jimbo. And we've said to Sally that we *will* pay the third instalment to her when it falls due later this year."

"So she won't be such a poor girl, after all," remarked Jack, but it wasn't clear whether he was being sardonic or simply stating a fact.

"Mm," was all that Neville said in response before he resumed, rubbing his hands together. "Okay, people, let's move on to more positive things. Market Surveys UK. Some of you will know all the story and some of you only parts of it, but let me recap on where we are with the company.

"First of all, there is now only one company. All the subsidiary companies, like Market Surveys Scotland, have gone, their dealings subsumed by MSUK. We're all employed by MSUK. That's the company we own shares in. And that's the company we'll be trading as. The only exception to that is Market Surveys Northern Ireland over in Belfast, which I own outright and which operates completely separately from MSUK.

"So moving on to our respective roles. I'll start with myself. I'm going to be bowing out of the operational side of the business and using the title of Chairman. Although it'll be a part-time role with a less hands-on approach, I'll still be very much involved in overseeing the company. But I'll have more time to concentrate on my TA duties, which have been expanding of late.

"And, of course," he joked, indicating Izzy's swollen belly, "as the politicians put it, I'll have more time to spend with my family."

He paused there while everyone took time to smile at a radiant-looking Izzy.

"Okay, so next up is yer man himself, Jack Lamb. Jack will formally become Managing Director of MSUK. As Dan has often pointed out to us in recent months, Jack has been more or less fulfilling that role for a long time, but now he'll be able to concentrate on it full-time..."

Jack seemed unable to contain himself. "Just to elaborate," he said, interrupting Neville's flow, "I'll be spending a lot of time on infrastructure matters, making sure we have the right infrastructure as the company continues to grow..."

"Thanks, Jack," Neville interrupted Jack in turn. "Now we come to Dan, the man. Our Dan here has the new title of Director of Operations. He'll be looking after *all* the executive teams from now on, not just the Social Research Team. It'll be quite an undertaking, but we're sure he's going to make a big success of it. And one of his first tasks will be to find a replacement for me down in Bristol. Unlike the situation when Sian left Cardiff, Bristol doesn't have a deputy I can hand the reins over to. So good luck with that one, Dan."

Dan simply smiled and nodded his acknowledgement.

"And last but not least, we come to the three ladies, who are not only shareholders of the company, but who will shortly also be Directors in their own right. Shelley becomes Director of Finance & Administration, Maisie becomes Director of Fieldwork and young Trish becomes Director of Data Processing & Analysis. Welcome to the Board, ladies."

All three followed Dan's example by smiling and nodding.

"Okay, well obviously this is our first Board meeting and it's been necessarily brief. We'll meet regularly from now on. I haven't decided yet if that'll be monthly or bi-monthly. But next time we come together we'll do things more fully, looking at the financial position and hearing reports from each of you. But I can't promise that Izzy will be with me – she'll probably have other matters to attend to."

Izzy beamed radiantly again.

"All right then, unless anybody has anything else, I'll finish off today's meeting with a couple of things I think you should all be aware of."

No-one spoke; not even Jack.

"Fine. Well, the first item concerns IT. With all the rapid advances in technology these days and with our increasing reliance on external IT consultants, we've come to the conclusion that we must put in place our own in-house IT expertise – and quickly. As I speak, Jack and Dan are jointly working on recruiting an IT Manager. They'll hopefully have made good progress on that by the next time we meet. And as soon as the IT Manager is in place, they'll get to work on developing an all-singing, all-dancing website for MSUK. Exciting times, people.

"And so to the very last item, which is about a change of auditors. I have to say I'm no longer happy with Alan, the chap we've been using over all these years. Alan used to be Shelley's boss, and as Shelley will tell you he's a lovely man. But he's like an old woman these days, so he is, going on about our cash flow and how much we're spending, but totally ignoring the fact that we've never been more profitable. I actually had to talk him out of qualifying our last set of accounts – our best set ever, by the way. No, I think the company has outgrown the wee man. So I'm now on the hunt for a new firm. Jack has recommended a couple of firms here in Glasgow who I'll be getting in touch with..."

Dan wasn't paying attention to Neville's tirade. He was too busy congratulating himself on the success of his strategy. Neville's hands-off role as Chairman, Jack formally becoming MD, him taking over the whole executive function, the three other Director appointments, even the recruitment of an IT Manager – all of it had been part of his strategy, his ideas, the seeds planted with Neville and Jack in the early days and then carefully nurtured with a combination of flattery and common sense over many months. With both Neville and Jack side-lined, he now had the complete earning resources of the company in his grasp – to mould into his way of working, to grow and ultimately to make more profitable. His lingering sadness over Jimbo's death aside, today was a glorious new beginning for him.

Chapter Fifteen

Glasgow, 2004

"Right at this moment, Neville, you couldnae sell your company for a penny. It's no' even worth that much."

Dan didn't know which of them he despised most. The sweaty, corpulent Glaswegian in the three-piece suit who had spoken those words. Or his two ugly sons who sat on either side of him, gloating like vultures. Or the bald-headed, obsequious Chairman of the company to whom the words were addressed. Or the lanky, smug-looking Managing Director who was the cause of the problem. Or the emptyheaded Financial Director who, but for her gormlessness, could have put a stop to it.

What he did know was that this was the last place on Earth he wanted to be. He was tired, drawn and very, very angry. Sight of the terrified expressions on the faces of Maisie and Trish added to his anger. But he needed to keep his cool, to endure the meeting and listen to the fat man, and then to do whatever it was going to take to preserve the company and his livelihood.

Yes, the gang was all there again. With barely a year having elapsed since their inaugural meeting, the shareholders were back in the boardroom, being told by McCash Senior of McCash & Sons, Chartered Accountants, Glasgow, that their company was about to go down the tubes.

"It's as simple as this," the fat man continued. "You owe the bank three hundred thousand. But the bank have seen your latest accounts, so they ken you have insufficient reserves to cover the debt. God knows what you've been doing to deplete your reserves to such an extent. The bank say they've been warning you about the situation for many months. Now they've lost patience with you. Unless you can convince them otherwise, they're on the verge of calling in their debt and making you bankrupt. And they'll only be convinced if this Board comes up with proposals for immediate, drastic and painful action."

Dan nodded. That was almost word-for-word how Alma had summed things up for him the night before, except that she had also established how and why the reserves had been depleted. Her conclusions came not long after Neville's phone call, urging Dan to drop everything and get on the train to Glasgow first thing the next day to attend an emergency Board meeting with the company's newly appointed auditors.

"We're in deep shit with the bank," Neville had said, panic in his voice. "Jack has just told me they're demanding repayment of their overdraft. Three hundred grand. Three hundred grand we don't have. We're in serious trouble, Dan."

Dan couldn't understand why the bank would behave that way. Business was booming. Turnover was greater than ever. And the executive teams were turning a handsome profit. He just couldn't understand it, but Neville wouldn't or couldn't elaborate, claiming to have other phone calls to make. So Dan dug out his copies of the company's final accounts for the three previous financial years and sought the benefit of Alma's accountancy expertise.

It didn't take Alma more than fifteen minutes to figure out what had been going on.

"The first problem can be found on the Balance Sheets for the three years," she explained as they sat side-by-side at the dining room table with the accounts spread out in front of them. "You can see that the company's reserves have reduced dramatically over the period – from about three hundred and fifty thousand at the beginning of 2001, which is here, to just under one hundred and ten thousand by the close of 2003, here. The difference is two hundred and forty thousand, which just happens to be the same amount I understand the company paid over to Jimbo to get his shares back.

"Now, I know the difference should have been more than offset by the profits that were supposed to be ploughed back into the company, the fifty per cent share of your team's profits. But as you can see it appears that nothing has been added to the reserves.

"So the question is: where have those profits gone? Well, a close examination of the three Profit and Loss Accounts reveals all. Let's start with the one for 2001. If I remember correctly, that was the year your team received over a hundred thousand in dividends and paid an equivalent amount back into the company – or thought you did. And I'm sure you told me that Jack Lamb's team didn't receive any dividends that year because they made a big loss. But have a look at this item here called *Dividends Paid.* It's more than *two* hundred thousand, exactly double what it should be. I think you'll find it's the same pattern in 2002 and 2003. That's where the profits went, I'm afraid, Dan."

Dan checked the *Dividends Paid* figures for 2002 and 2003, looked at Alma and nodded solemnly. He couldn't believe it, the enormity of it. He sat there shaking his head, not saying anything. Then at last he exclaimed:

"You stupid, stupid, gutless man, Neville! You've been giving in to the sleekit, petulant bastard, paying his team the same dividends as mine. And for three fucking years in a row!"

He suddenly remembered hearing Maisie complain a while ago about Jack's executives strutting around the office and bragging about the dividend payments they had just received, but he knew that couldn't be the case, so he dismissed it as gossip.

He also remembered his manners.

"Thank you, Al. Thank you for taking the time to do that, hen," he said, still trying to come to terms with the scale of the duplicity. "But surely Shelley would have known what Neville and Jack were up to. Surely she would have realised how dangerous it was."

Alma smiled. "You'd think so, wouldn't you? But the way I see it, either she agreed with what they were doing or she's just plain stupid. Personally, I'd go for the latter. Like I told you a long time ago, the woman's nothing but a jumped-up bookkeeper."

"Maybe a bit of both, hen – vindictive, as well as stupid. By all accounts, she seems to spend a lot of time in the office in a huddle with Jack Lamb."

Then something Neville had said at that first shareholders' meeting returned to Dan. *I think the company has outgrown the wee man.* Neville was questioning the competence of their previous auditor, wanting to get rid of him. Dan had been listening with only half an ear back then, but last night, in the light of Alma's discoveries, Neville's remarks made sense to him. Had "the wee man" found out or suspected what was going on? Was that why Neville was so desperate to replace him?

And here Dan was the following morning, watching and listening to Jack's recommended replacement mop his expansive brow and continue to berate his audience. Dan thought the wide pinstriped suit, the large flowery tie and the gravelly voice combined to make McCash Senior look more like a Mafia boss than an accountant. At any other time, he would have found the sight of him comical. But today there was no room for humour; what he had to say was deadly serious.

"It seems to us that you've actually made two fatal errors. As if spending nearly all your reserves wisnae enough, over the years you've systematically failed to agree a higher overdraft limit. You've probably had the three hundred grand limit for many years. For a company your size, the limit should be double that figure at least. You should have negotiated an increase with the bank a long time ago."

As if he was demanding an explanation from her, Neville turned to Shelley, who gave the merest of shrugs and said nothing. The blank look on her face incensed Dan. *Useless, useless cunt*, he hissed under his breath.

"But surely the bank realises that the situation is only temporary?"

Neville asked McCash in a weak, pleading voice. "A couple of big cheques from clients in the post tomorrow and we'd be all sorted again. Couldn't we just re-negotiate the overdraft limit with the bank right now?"

"Like I explained earlier, Neville, it's too late for that. Yes, your cash flow could be sorted tomorrow. But only until the next time. And the next time. And the time after that. Until it can't be sorted any more.

"And, yes, we'll help you re-negotiate the overdraft limit – once we're able to convince the bank to work with you again. That's what we're here for, to get you out of this hole you've dug for yourselves. But we can only do that if you take the actions we're about to propose."

McCash paused there to wipe his brow again.

"Okay then, down tae brass tacks. The first thing the bank is gonnae look for is a cash commitment from each of the Directors of the company. They'll want to see you use your own money to significantly reduce or even wipe out the overdraft. Now, paying off the full whack of three hundred grand is probably too ambitious, so I'm going to suggest a figure of two hundred thousand. It disnae matter how you dae it individually – whether it's out of your savings or extending your mortgage or borrowing from a relation – but if yous can jointly pull the cash together we'll be halfway to getting you back into business with the bank. The cash would be treated in the accounts as Directors' loans, of course, and would be repayable to the individuals once the company was back on an even keel."

Before the scale of what was being asked for had time to sink in with the others, Neville was there with a suggestion to them.

"I suppose we should divvy up the cash according to the percentage of the company's shares we each own. With my fifty-five per cent, I would have to pay over a hundred grand, but I should be able to come up with that sum quite quickly. What do you think, people? Is that how we do it?"

There were mutters of assent all round. Dan felt deeply sorry for Maisie and Trish, each of whom would have to find six thousand pounds almost overnight, but he smiled to himself when he realised that slimy Jack would need to fork out a cool fifty grand. Perhaps that was why the latter was unusually quiet; he didn't look so smug now. As for himself, fortunately he and Alma had sufficient savings available to cover his eleven per cent share of the two hundred thousand. The only downside was that they wouldn't be able to plan any more holidays abroad for a while.

"Good," grunted McCash. "I'll be able to relay that news to the bank on your behalf. But now we come to requirement number two. Not only will the bank be looking for an immediate cash commitment, they'll also want to hold some form of security over each of you in case of problems in the future. And their preferred form of security, I'm afraid to tell you, is the property you own personally or jointly with a partner. Now dinnae get too concerned about this. It's something banks rarely resort to, but it keeps them happy to have it on file. It's a formality, really, signifying your further commitment. All you'll need to do is sign a pro forma that we'll–"

Before McCash could finish his last sentence, Neville was there again with another question.

"There's a townhouse – an office building – in Belfast that I own outright. I'd prefer to use that as my security, if that's okay."

That's right, you wanker, thought Dan, *make sure your mansion down in Bristol isn't on the fucking line. Unlike everyone else's homes.*

"That'll no' be a problem, Neville," McCash replied. "As for the rest of yous, go home the night and discuss this with your wives or husbands or what-have-you. But you'll need to emphasise that it's a vital requirement. The securities will need to be completed very soon – within the next week or so."

On the understanding that the meeting was drawing to a close, papers were being shuffled and chairs pushed back. But it wasn't over yet, not until the fat man was finished. And his next statement had everyone sitting still again.

"Last but no' least is requirement number three. The bank will also want to be reassured that the company is gonnae continue as a profitable business. So you'll need to dae something that'll reassure them. I see from your last accounts that you carry a hefty amount of overheads, consisting mostly of expenditure on staff–"

"Well, market research is a staff-intensive business," Jack butted in unhelpfully.

Dan shook his head. *You just couldn't help yourself, could you, Mister fucking Know-it-all?*

"That may well be the case, Jack," McCash shrugged, "but what I'm proposing is that you should give the bank the reassurance they're looking for by showing them you're in the process of reducing your overheads. I'd recommend that the reduction is not less than ten per cent. So go through the books and cut out any unnecessary expenditure until you reach that target. Inevitably, it'll mean that some of your staff will have to go. Like I said at the start, it's gonnae be painful. The expenditure reduction is a longer-term requirement, though, so take your time over it and get it right."

The cash commitment and the security on the house hadn't surprised Dan; Alma had predicted those as well last night. But she hadn't figured on any staff having to be dismissed. That measure was probably over the top. And the worst part was that they would pick on the youngest members of staff, the ones who deserved it least, while the useless Shelleys of this world carried on untouched. Dan felt as if he had been kicked in the stomach. He needed a cigarette. He needed some air. He needed out of there.

As he got up to go, the bold Neville was taking charge again.

"Okay, people, obviously we'll have to meet again – and soon – to go over that last requirement in more detail. I'll be back in touch once I fix a date for the meeting. But in the meantime please have a good think about your own staff, about anyone you could live without. Thanks to McCash & Sons, it looks like we will survive and bounce back leaner and wiser."

Before he left, Dan nodded curtly at the fat man and his ugly sons, and sympathetically at Maisie and Trish, but he couldn't bear to look at any of the remaining trio, the perpetrators of that day's mess. With his back to them, he simply raised a hand and called out, "I'll phone you later, Neville."

Out on the noisy, crowded Shawlands pavements, he decided to forego a taxi and walk to Queen Street Station. It was a long trek, but it would help to clear his head and build his resolve to face the months ahead.

Alma and he had talked late into the night, reviewing his future options as far as MSUK was concerned. They concluded that the company was worth fighting for, that with the right amount of effort it could go places. This business with the bank was a temporary setback, a problem caused by a hangover from the previous regime: the seventy/thirty split of overheads between the two executive divisions. With all the executive resources now under Dan's control, the split was no longer relevant, so the problem would not recur. It was up to him to use those resources to turn MSUK into a bigger and more profitable company, while at the same time keeping a wary eye open for any further shenanigans by the terrible trio.

Besides, they had gotten used to the high life and needed the big salary and the juicy dividends from the company if they were to continue to enjoy that life. They hadn't long moved into Edinburgh's prestigious New Town, having purchased the basement flat of a Georgian townhouse. The flat was similar to their previous one in the West End, except it was larger and spread over two levels. It had a private courtyard at the front and a little garden for their exclusive use at the rear. The property was worth half a million in the current market. And it came with a sizeable mortgage, which they could easily afford. They could also afford the best of furniture and furnishings. And the expensive clothes and jewellery. Not to mention up to four holidays a year in locations across Europe and Asia.

As he walked and thought about their life, Dan's resolve hardened. Yes, he would suck up the present difficulties and continue to work with Neville and Jack, but only for his and Alma's benefit. He was in his fifties now, though, and he sure as hell wasn't going to work with those awful people for another ten years. He also needed to develop his exit strategy.

Chapter Sixteen

London, 2005

Dan found a seat in the departure lounge of London City Airport, switched on his mobile phone, took a sip of his celebratory beer and thanked God for tall, blonde, thirtysomething Englishwomen with posh voices and double-barrelled names. Well, one tall, blonde Englishwoman, in particular. Vicky Spencer-Smith was Neville's replacement in the Bristol office whom Dan had recruited about eighteen months earlier. Normally, he would have been put off by the voice, the name, the private girls' school education, but Vicky turned out to be a down-to-earth lass, who swore like a trooper to boot. Naturally, they became instant buddies. With a background in mathematics, Vicky was also extremely clever, wrote wonderful proposals and excelled at presentations. Only hours earlier, she had employed the last of those qualities to secure MSUK's biggest ever contract.

He looked at his phone and wondered who he should call first to pass on the good news. By rights, it should be the Managing Director. But he remembered an almost identical situation the year before. He and Geoff were in a taxi travelling back to East Midlands Airport, having just been informed by the local Development Agency that they had been successful in tendering for a major survey, worth three-quarters of a million, the company's biggest contract at that time. His first call from the taxi was to Jack, whose reaction to what in reality was a lifesaver for MSUK was lukewarm, to say the least. It felt very much as if Jack was peeved because it wasn't *him*, the big man, the hero, who had won the contract and saved the company.

No, he wouldn't call Jack at all this time. He reckoned that by now Vicky would have informed the girls in Bristol. It wouldn't take long before the news was relayed by them to the other offices. So he would let Jack find out through the company's very efficient grapevine.

Not that he and Jack were at loggerheads. On the contrary, they had been co-operating closely ever since the big fright from the bank, ever since the subsequent staff pogrom, in which he had been forced to take part, when mostly poor, defenceless youngsters across the country were told they were no longer required by MSUK. After that dirty business, he had requested a meeting with Jack, a meeting to clear the air, at which he confronted the man with evidence of his role in depleting the reserves. Jack wasn't contrite in the least. He was still bitter about the seventy/thirty split of overheads. He still insisted that the arrangement had deprived him and his team of a rightful share of the company's profits and that he had simply taken measures to rectify the unfairness.

Recognising that they wouldn't be able to move on until the matter was resolved, Dan came up with a way out of the impasse.

"Okay, Jack, we'll have to agree to disagree on that," he said. "But let's go a step further. Let's take the issue and put it in a box. And let's lock the box and throw away the key. Just imagine we're both down at the Clyde right now and we're chucking the key into the river. That's it. It's gone. Neither of us can open that box. So neither of us will be able to mention the issue ever again."

Dan's suggestion seemed to work. He and Jack did move on, jointly setting about the development of a stronger and more profitable business. But the issue locked away in the box, although now out of mind, was unlikely to be forgotten by either of them.

As he had promised to do back at that initial shareholders' meeting, Jack worked with his usual gusto on a range of infrastructure issues, modernising the company's personnel policies, its quality control procedures and, most importantly, its computer systems network. An inveterate bullshitter, he also succeeded in raising MSUK's image within the market research industry. Having discovered that the highly influential Market Research Society had ranked MSUK among the top twenty market research organisations in the UK, he even managed to blag his way on to the Board of the Society,

For his part, Dan concentrated his efforts on the executives formerly under Jack's control, introducing them to his system of personal turnover targets, regular monitoring and frequent encouragement. Egged on by Jack, who at one point trawled the Internet to come up with a list of twenty reasons why individual sales targets should never be set, there was much opposition initially from the executives in Glasgow to the concept of personal targets. But Dan ignored Jack's list and persisted. Soon the targets were in operation in Glasgow and elsewhere. And soon the turnover was rising across all the executive teams in England, Scotland and Wales. A few big commissions later, particularly the biggest of all from the East Midlands Development Agency, and it wasn't long before MSUK's *annus horribilis* was left far behind. Nor was it long before the Directors' Loans were repaid (with interest), the bank withdrew the securities it held over the Directors' personal properties, and the offices began to employ additional staff, in some cases the same people who had been dismissed only a short time ago.

And while all that was going on, Jack and Dan met with Neville every month to review progress on their respective initiatives and, more crucially, to keep a close eye on the company's finances; all three had vowed they were never going to get caught out by the bank again. They worked effectively as a team, even calling themselves the Senior Management Team. Together, they established MSUK's first presence in London; it was a small office staffed by only two executives, but it was a start, a foothold.

The only point of contention arose when Jack, not satisfied with the multitude of other tasks he was working on, decided that he would embark on a round of regular visits to all the offices outside Glasgow, ostensibly to troubleshoot accommodation, administration and computer system difficulties. None of the local managers were happy with these visits; they were a nuisance at best, an interference at worst. Having experienced a very similar situation in his time with the SNHC, where visits to area offices around Scotland by a highly autocratic, ex-military General Manager became a source of amusement, rather than something to be dreaded, Dan advised his managers to take a more relaxed attitude.

"Make him welcome, give him a cup of coffee, take him out to lunch, butter him up, tell him what needs improved," he often joked with them. "He'll be gone before you know it. And remember, while we get on and do the real work, the poor man has to deal with things like the company's health and safety policy. He needs a wee bit of excitement in his life."

In truth, though, knowing the man's megalomaniac tendencies, Dan was fearful that before long Jack would overstep the purpose of his visits and begin to encroach on his side of the business. It was a problem bubbling under the surface, something to be watched closely.

Still undecided over who to call first – it was a toss-up between Neville and Maisie – Dan lifted his glass to take another sip of his beer when his mobile rang and decided for him.

"Think of the devil and he's sure to appear," he said to Neville.

"Eh?"

"I was on the point of phoning you, Neville," he lied, "and suddenly here you are."

"Ah, right, I see. Where are you just now?"

"London City Airport, waiting for the flight back to Edinburgh."

"Right. Well, by pure chance, I was on the phone to Meg in the Bristol office when Vicky called Charlotte with the good news. Fuckin' brilliant, so it is! The GLC, isn't it? Charlotte says it's worth millions. You are the fuckin' man, Dan!"

"The GLC was abolished years ago, Neville. No, it's the GLA, the Greater London Authority. You know, where Ken Livingstone is the

Mayor."

"Ah, of course."

"Well, they're awarding us a two-year contract to begin with to carry out pan-London social attitude surveys every quarter. We'll be asking households about crime, housing, traffic management, parking, the Tube, the environment – in fact, you name it and we'll be asking about it. And, yes, the contract will be worth a couple of million at least and could be extended beyond the two years if we do a good job."

"Jesus, Dan, you're a fuckin' genius, so you are."

"Well, to be perfectly honest, none of this is down to me. All the credit goes to Maisie and Vicky. Maisie came down here earlier in the week to convince the GLA that we could mount a big enough interviewer team and that the team would include the right number of speakers of ethnic minority languages, that sort of thing. Then today Vicky gave a stormer of a presentation. She had them eating out of her hands. I wasn't needed at all. Just a fuckin' bystander.

"You know, Neville, that lassie Vicky could run the company. She should be promoted. Her and Geoff, perhaps. Give both of them some shares and seats on the Board. The company would be all the better for it."

It wasn't the first time Dan had made that suggestion. But the ensuing silence on this occasion was a sure-fire sign that Neville didn't agree with the suggestion. It was also a sure-fire sign that Jack had been there, poisoning Neville's mind about Vicky and Geoff, both of whom had had numerous run-ins with Jack and neither of whom had any time for the man. *Sleekit big cunt*, thought Dan before breaking the silence.

"Anyway, this contract with the GLA is certain to push us up the Market Research Society's league table. Might get us into the top ten, you never know. That's bound to make us even more attractive to potential buyers."

"I hear what you're saying, Dan. And you may well be right. I think I'll email that chap David Green with the news. I told you about him, didn't I? He's the Chairman of the Cresta Group plc. He aims to create a big research and marketing conglomerate, so he's been going around buying up all sorts of companies – ad agencies, PR agencies, market research agencies. He's interested in MSUK – he's following our progress, so he says – because of our UK-wide presence. But we'll see. It's early days yet. I'll email him anyway."

"Aye, do that, please, Neville. Anyway, I better get on and let Maisie have the news before my flight's called. I'll catch up with you soon, no doubt."

"Okay, byeee. And well done again."

When Neville had ended the call, Dan couldn't help smiling to himself. Not about the GLA contract. But about his exit strategy. He had often heard Neville and Jimbo talk about eventually selling the company. So at one of those regular Senior Management Team meetings he had reintroduced the possibility of selling. As expected, Jack was cold to the idea, but Neville was extremely interested – and that's what mattered. At another point, he asked Neville outright the *least* amount he would accept for the company.

"I wouldn't let it go for anything less than four million," replied the bold Neville.

That was the trigger for Neville to begin looking in earnest for potential buyers. Even Jack couldn't object. As the Americans would say, he could do the math. Twenty-five per cent of four million. A cool one million pounds. And that was the least he could expect from any sale.

Dan could do the math as well. His eleven per cent of the sale figure would provide a handsome retirement sum for Alma and him. They had fallen in love with Venice a long time before, they visited the city often and they had chosen to see in the Millennium there. They had dreams of retiring to *La Serenissima*, the most beautiful city in the world, growing old together while Venice sank gracefully into the lagoon. It was a romantic notion, but one that was fast becoming a reality.

Chapter Seventeen

Glasgow, 2007

Jack closed the drawer of his desk, leaned back in his chair, stretched out his long legs and began the operation. *Thinking time*, he said to himself.

Ping! went the screen of his laptop.

From where Jack sat, with only the receptionist and the main door to his rear, almost the whole of the open-plan office was laid out before him in a wide arc. He had chosen that strategic location for his desk so that he could keep an eye on the staff and their comings and goings. As far as he was concerned, that ability to quietly survey all those people – *his* people in *his* empire – was what made everything worthwhile.

"It gives me a great sense of achievement," he once confided to Neville. "It's what gets me up in the morning."

He had been annoyed with himself afterwards for opening up to Neville like that – he had imbibed an uncharacteristic third beer that night, two beers being his normal limit at social gatherings, especially those involving the staff – because he knew that at every opportunity when his back was turned Neville would repeat his outpouring to others in the company.

Ping! went the coat-stand at the side of the next desk down, where Polly, his PA, sat with her back to him.

It was the midpoint between the morning break and lunchtime. Save for the soft tapping of a dozen or so keyboards, the rustle of papers here and there and the odd murmured phone call, the office was hushed at that hour. *Thinking time*, Jack repeated to himself. Now was an ideal opportunity to plan the structure of the presentation that he would give at the forthcoming staff conference.

Scanning the series of desks ahead of him and to his right, he was pleased to see that all the heads were down. He liked it when everyone was busy and there was no overt skiving anywhere. As usual, though, the only blot on an otherwise perfect landscape was that bloody room down there on his left. It was the only enclosed room in the whole office. When the company moved its head office to larger premises a few years back, the room was meant to be *his*; as Managing Director, he was supposed to have his own private space. However, despite Neville's protestations, he had steadfastly declined the room, insisting instead on being placed among his people. That was when he had let it slip to Neville about what got him up in the morning. A bad mistake.

Ping! went the back of Polly's chair.

Jack didn't notice the shudder that ran through Polly. Nor did he see the signals that were exchanged between Polly and Trish, who sat a few desks away. He was too caught up thinking about the private room. He had wanted to use it as a storage room, but Maisie had demanded it, nagging him about it every day for weeks on end.

"Can I remind you, Jack, that I'm the Director of Fieldwork with responsibility for the large majority of the staff in this place?" had been her daily mantra. "You must see that I need to have my own office so that I can deal with personnel matters in complete confidence."

He had had to agree with the bitch, of course. Another bad mistake. He had only given in to her because the room was glass-fronted and he thought he would be able to see directly into it from his vantage point. It hadn't occurred to him that she would keep the blinds closed all day – deliberately, in his opinion, to block off his view. As a further insult to him, the door to the room was closed this morning. He knew that she was ensconced in there with some of her minions, but he didn't have a clue about what they were all up to. Letting her have the room had been another bad mistake, all right.

Ping! went the glass plate on the wall adjacent to his desk. Mounted on that exact spot so that it was visible to any visitor to his desk, the plate was a trophy from the local enterprise agency. The words *Fastest Growing Business, Small to Medium Size Category, 2001* were inscribed in fake gold leaf on it. Although well out-of-date now, the trophy reminded Jack every morning that it was he who single-handedly had steered the company from its third-rate origins to its present success.

Polly shuddered again, stood up, collected her handbag and walked towards the exit. Trish copied her actions moments later. With his eyes still fixed on the closed door to Maisie's room, Jack hardly noticed the two ladies leaving. Not to worry, he nodded to himself, Maisie would be getting her comeuppance soon enough. He would be getting rid of her and a few others before long. That posh git of a Research Director down in Winchester for a start. Lord Snooty Hamish had annoyed him too many times now. He was always out of line, seldom followed procedures and seemed just to do his own thing as if *he* were the bloody MD! And his office was always a tip – stuff stuck up all over the walls with Blu-Tack, in spite of instructions to the contrary. Well, all his misdemeanours were detailed in Jack's notebook, along with possible scenarios for his dismissal. It was the same for Vicky, Dan's pet in Bristol, who never knew when to keep her big mouth closed. And Maisie and all the other square pegs and deadwood in the company. He had recorded lots of evidence in that little black book in case it was needed at any future employment tribunals; something he had learned to do after being ejected from the last place by his so-called fellow-Directors...

Jack seemed to flinch from that last memory. Giving the slightest of jerks, he drew his gaze away from Maisie's door and began to contemplate the backs of his hands instead, unaware that three other staff members were in the act of slipping away from their desks to follow Polly and Trish out of the office. Anyway, he resumed his thoughts, his little black book, the dismissals, the tribunals: they were all for another day.

Right now, he needed everyone on board as he embarked on the next phase of his strategy to grow the company… which brought him right back to the business of the staff conference.

Ping! went Polly's keyboard.

Yes, he nodded to himself again, the first phase of what he described as his "strategy for growth" had been a resounding success. Over a year ago, he had introduced a brand new logo, a new website, new letterheads, new business cards, new signage – the lot. It was a new *identity* for the company, really; smart and modern and eye-catching. And he had succeeded in getting all the staff – and clients – to embrace it. He got the idea for it when he attended a course run by the enterprise agency. He commissioned a design company immediately afterwards. That was twenty grand well spent, in his opinion.

Now it was time for phase two. He had decided a few months ago that the new logo on its own wasn't enough. It needed a catchy strapline to complement it. So he had gone back to the design company and asked them to come up with some ideas for one. *Solid thinking* was the idea they had recommended and he had readily accepted. It was exactly what he had been looking for and worth every penny of the extra five grand he had paid them.

"The word *Solid* denotes the experience, professionalism and dependability of the company, Jack," they had explained in their special design-speak, which he always found stimulating (or "sexy", as they would say), "while the word *thinking* conveys the company's creativity and its depth of expertise."

Jack smiled. He thought there was a perfect symmetry to those two words. He hoped that Neville, Dan, the others on the Board, the Research Directors and all the rest of the morons would be able to see that symmetry, that balance, when he unveiled the strapline at the conference. But how to unveil it? That was the question.

Ping! went the silver frame of the photograph that was perched at the end of Jack's desk. The photograph had been taken at the last staff conference, when he had launched the company's new identity. Wanting to appear more distinguished and more *in charge*, he had worn his white suit that day and he had grown a beard for the occasion, which he hadn't removed since then. Jack frequently admired the photograph. He felt that it portrayed him as proud and quietly confident in his white suit and beard. With the whole of the staff, almost eighty-strong of them from across the UK, standing four-deep at some distance behind him, he also thought that it made him look like a giant among them, like Gulliver among the Lilliputians.

He had already organised the date, location and format of the conference. It would be held in London at the same venue as last year, a fairly modest hotel near Russell Square, which was reasonably central. He had chosen London again, not because it was an exciting place to go to, but because everyone outside of London could get there cheaply by budget airline. The downside was that they had to get up very early in the morning to catch the flight in and they usually had to hang about the airport until quite late for the return flight. But neither of those inconveniences had ever bothered Jack; not when the flights at those hours cost next to nothing.

As far as the format was concerned, he had decided that the conference that year should take place over two days, rather than one. It would begin just after lunchtime on the first day and would go on until early evening, when there would be a brief interval to allow people to freshen up before the conference dinner in the hotel. Then it would reconvene at nine o'clock on the morning of the second day, closing at lunchtime. Jack intended the early start on day two to discourage the excessive drinking that had gone on after previous conference dinners. More particularly, he sought to deter Neville and Dan from dragging half the staff over to that damned all-night bar in Covent Garden. He most certainly wanted to avoid a repeat of last year's disgrace, when he had observed Neville, Dan and a group of other drunks staggering into the hotel at five am, just as he was leaving it to catch the flight back to Glasgow.

Ping! went the back of the monitor on the desk directly across the corridor. Jack noticed that Harvey, the desk's occupant, was no longer there. Probably gone to the loo, he decided, before examining the backs of his hands again.

He already had a fair idea of the conference agenda over the two days. On day one, there would be his own PowerPoint presentation, of course, when he would give an overview of the company's current financial position and its future trading prospects. Then each of the Board Directors in turn would give a presentation on his or her area of responsibility. Finally, the Research Directors would provide brief accounts of what was happening in their respective localities. It was all the usual stuff, really, except that he would be using his presentation somehow to introduce *Solid thinking*.

Jack paused for a moment, suddenly remembering something. Yes, except also that he had decided not to include an address from the Chairman. What was the point of letting Neville say anything? he asked himself. The man wasn't even *productive*, was he? Okay, so he was the "majority shareholder", a phrase that he frequently bleated to Jack, but it wasn't him who had turned his failing company round, was it? Nor was it Dan or any of the other Board Directors, no matter how much they all claimed to be instrumental in the company's growth. The very idea of it! No, it was all down to yours truly. His ideas. His vision. His leadership. The company really belonged to *him* now, which was another reason for putting a gag on Neville; everyone at the conference needed to understand that it was him, Jack Lamb, not their lazy Chairman, who was firmly in charge.

Right, Jack snorted, he would tell Neville that the agenda was too full to include anything from the Chairman on it. If Neville objected, he would do what he always did to get his own way: he would threaten to resign. The threat was always enough for Neville to cave in; the man knew what side his bread was buttered on. Neville Brown. N.B. for No Balls. No Balls Neville. That's what he had heard some of the staff call him. And who was he to disagree with them? A tight, little smile appeared on his face.

Ping! went Jack's wastepaper bin.

The smile disappeared. Anyway, he thought sarcastically, No Balls Neville would have plenty of opportunity to talk his usual rubbish on day two of the conference. He hadn't worked out the details yet, but he planned a sort of brainstorming session, in which the staff would be asked to come up with some new ideas for marketing the company. Sure, he would take away a few of those ideas – one or two, maybe – and promise to develop them, but that was all. He didn't want anyone to get carried away, thinking that they could significantly influence the running of the company. That was his role – and his role only. Oh, yeah, he had experienced staff democracy in action in the last place, and see what happened. It turned into a management fucking buyout! And the first thing that the bastards did was to fire him! No, there would be no tail wagging the dog in this company; he would stamp on anything remotely resembling it.

Ping! went Jack's screen again. A slide of his draft PowerPoint presentation occupied the screen. The cursor sat halfway down the slide, blinking at him, reminding him that he still had to decide how and where to incorporate *Solid thinking*.

It occurred to Jack in a flash, as all his good ideas did, that he could introduce the strapline *without actually saying anything*. A slide with nothing but the words *Solid thinking* emblazoned across its centre could pop up intermittently throughout his presentation – whenever he paused, perhaps. Each time it popped up, the slide could linger for five seconds, say, before fading away. And when it appeared some rousing music could play. Wagner, maybe. A snatch of *Ride of the Valkyries*. That would do it! And every time the slide was there he would say absolutely nothing, pretending to ignore it, just letting the image – the *concept* – register with the audience in the same way as subliminal messages. Afterwards, when he had finished his presentation and invited questions, someone was bound to ask what *Solid thinking* was all about. Then he could launch into a full explanation. Perfect!

Jack paused. But who would ask the question? He didn't want Neville opening his big mouth, nor did he want any sarcasm from toffee-nosed Hamish or mouthy Vicky or any of the other smartarses in the company. No, he would have to control that bit by briefing someone beforehand to do it. Shelley would be the best person; he could rely on her, he could trust her.

Oblivious to the fact that half the desks were empty now and that the office was even quieter than before, Jack looked across to the desk in the far corner, where Shelley, the Director of Finance & Administration, sat in deep concentration in front of her computer screen, her glasses perched on the end of her nose. He liked Shelley a great deal. In fact, she was the *only* person whom he could trust, whom he could really confide in. He sighed. If he could live his life over again, he would want to marry her, not the self-important *prima donna* whom he shared a bed with. He sighed again, remembering that *she* would be coming to the conference dinner as well – she insisted on attending every staff get-together, as if she was Lady Fucking Bountiful – and that, as usual, he would have to keep an eye on the lush's drink intake.

Ping! went the ceiling above Jack's head.

Right, he said to himself, examining the backs of his hands once more. Operation over. And some solid thought about *Solid thinking* in the process. He grinned, amused by his clever play on words.

There was a small crowd outside at the front of the building. For the third or fourth time, Harvey detached himself from it and walked over to the window at the side of the main entrance, from where he had a clear view of the whole length of the open-plan office.

"It's okay, folks," he called to the others. "He's finished. He's putting his nail clippers back into the drawer. It's safe to go in now."

Polly stubbed out her cigarette.

"Thank God," she shivered. "It's freezing out here. But every time

I hear those clippers going, my flesh begins to crawl and I have to get out."

"You and me both," agreed Trish, who stood with her arms wrapped around herself.

"Tell you what?" said Harvey. "Next time, why don't we video it and put it on YouTube? That would embarrass the wanker."

Chapter Eighteen

Edinburgh, 2008

Jack says he's happy with it. When he saw that sentence in Neville's email, Dan knew for certain he had made the biggest mistake of his life. His hopes for the next day, his plans for the future, his dreams of a new life in *La Serenissima* – they all seemed to perish with those six words.

It was nine o'clock at night. He was sitting at his desk in his little study at home, staring at the screen of his laptop, staring at those words in the email, as if transfixed. He was desperate to act, to rewrite Neville's report before it was too late, but panic had set in. He couldn't think. He felt unwell. It had been a bad day. A bad night. In fact, it had been a bad six months, ever since that mad moment when he lost his temper and decided to change the game, to trust in fate, to gamble.

It was those visits of Jack's to what he called the "remote" offices that had done it for Dan. Back at the SNHC, the ex-military General Manager – Major-General Fucking Disaster, he was nicknamed by the staff – used to circulate a ten-page report to all the senior managers after each of his site visits. Jack's reports were similar in length, but sent in an email only to Dan. At first, Dan would respond good-naturedly to the points contained in the emails; they were trivia to him, but obviously important to Jack. But as time went on the tone of the emails grew more strident, more autocratic, more demanding; the trivia transformed into *instructions* to Dan. Gone was the concept of he and Dan working in partnership. Jack was demonstrating that he was no longer the Managing Director in name only, that he had assumed the full mantle of the position, that he was now firmly in charge.

Naturally, Dan complained to Neville about Jack's increasingly aggressive and interfering behaviour.

"I'll have a word with yer man and get him to wind his neck in," Neville promised, but nothing changed.

And then one night at his home, at about the same time as tonight, while he was in the middle of writing a report that was needed for the next day, Dan received another lengthy, abusive email from Jack. It was the last straw. He snapped. It took him less than a minute to decide what to do. He picked up the phone and spoke as calmly as he could to Neville.

"I'm sorry to say that I've come to the end of my tether with Jack. I've just received his latest missive after his trip to Winchester. He wants me to fire Hamish this time. The guy's fuckin' loony tunes, Neville. I've just to ignore the fact that Hamish pulls in several hundred grand in turnover every year.

"Anyway, here's a proposal for you to think about. I'd like to pull back from the operational side and let Jack have what he's always wanted, which is complete control of the executive teams. Let him fuckin' get on with it. I'd prefer to concentrate on strategic matters. There's a hundred things I've been itching to do from a strategic point of view, but have never had the time. Developing a much-needed database to help the executives put together shit-hot tenders, for a start. I could have a new title – I'm thinking of Director of Strategy.

"But knowing that the sale of the company is really the most important item on our agenda at the moment, I could also work in parallel to help you make the case to David Green at Cresta – prepare reports on your behalf, that sort of thing. And if the Cresta deal falls through, I could help you search for other potential buyers. All on the quiet, of course."

There were no objections from Neville. He agreed readily to Dan's proposal. Too readily, maybe, Dan thought afterwards. With Dan no longer involved in the day-to-day running of the company, perhaps Neville could envisage a quieter life for himself, one in which he wouldn't have to listen to Jack's constant griping about the executive teams. Dan didn't know if that was the case. Nor did he care – he just wanted to be away from the man's suffocating megalomania.

Dan also thought afterwards that he had possibly taken too big a risk in yielding his operations role to Jack. But his fears were lessened when he remembered that the executive teams practically ran themselves. Only months earlier, Vicky and Geoff had been promoted to the posts of Regional Director South and Regional Director North respectively, with Vicky becoming responsible for the teams in the south of England and Wales and Geoff managing the rest of the teams in the north of England and Scotland. The new posts had been created to ease the growing burden on Dan, acting as a buffer between him and the daily demands of the teams, and were now occupied by two very capable and reliable pairs of hands.

And then, of course, there was the other factor that minimised the risk – the sale of the company. By that time, Neville had succeeded in developing a good rapport with David Green. The man definitely was interested in buying MSUK, adding the company to his group's portfolio. Neville was certain an offer from Cresta was imminent; an offer, moreover, that would match, if not exceed, his minimum selling price of four million pounds. With any luck, therefore, the teams wouldn't have to suffer Jack's dictatorship for too long.

But luck deserted Dan on this occasion. His gamble didn't pay off. He wasn't prepared for the sheer speed and ferocity of Jack's vindictiveness. Nor was he prepared for Neville's utterly cowardly behaviour. Worst of all, he hadn't anticipated the true extent of Jack's business incompetence.

Within a day of receiving the news about Dan, Jack instructed all the Research Directors across the UK to attend an emergency meeting in Glasgow the following week. It turned out to be less of a meeting and more of a lecture by Jack, most of which he devoted to decrying Dan and criticising Dan's style of management. He also took the opportunity to abolish with immediate effect the operation of personal turnover targets, claiming he had always believed they were impractical. Dan became aware of all this, not because any of the Research Directors contacted him afterwards, but from a note of the proceedings that Jack typed and emailed to him the next day.

Following that email, Dan was removed from the circulation list of all communications within the company. The only information he was "permitted" to receive were the quarterly financial reports prepared by Shelley. But those reports, as well as always being late, were retrospective only, containing no financial projections for the months ahead. Denied the full picture of how the company was actually performing, Dan quickly sought Neville's help. Instead of remedying the matter there and then, however, Neville suggested a meeting with Jack, with him acting as referee. Dan duly turned up at the boardroom in Glasgow to find Jack seated at the far end of the table, with Neville, his "minder", sitting close by and with his laptop open in front of him, as if to provide added protection.

Dan chuckled to himself at the sight of Jack cowering in a corner. *Aye, he must have heard about the fight in the lift with Jimbo. Now the big streak of shite is scared I'm going to thump him as well.*

But he wasn't chuckling when he left the boardroom less than ten minutes later. He did confront Jack about his exclusion from important communications. Even though it was delivered from behind a laptop screen, Jack's response was emphatic.

"It's as simple as this, Dan. By excluding yourself from the company's operations, you automatically excluded yourself from any communications about those operations. What and how the executives are doing is no longer any of your business. We were sailing along, doing well together, and then, unaccountably, you decided to abandon ship. You only have yourself to blame for this."

Dan could see things clearly now The man was miffed, angry, still stinging from the hurt of being rejected. The idea of anyone actually deserting him was unbearable. *You poor, deluded cunt,* he thought.

"Is that it then?" he addressed Neville. "Are you just going to sit there and let him do this without saying a word? You know that I have as much right to the information as he has. You need to remember I'm the guy, not him, who put your company into profit and made it ripe for sale."

"I do remember that, Dan. And I'm more than grateful," Neville said meekly. "But on this occasion I have to agree with Jack. You really have excluded yourself. But that doesn't mean you and I can't continue to work together, especially on the business of selling the company."

When Dan got up to go, he noticed with relish a small shudder escape from Jack. But he left the room quietly, still unable to fathom the Svengali-like hold that Jack seemed to have over Neville.

Cut off from the company's day-to-day business and without any pressing work to do, Dan decided to take a holiday – a long holiday. He and Alma rented an apartment in Venice for six weeks. During their stay, they used the local shops and cooked and ate in the apartment, living like Venetian citizens, rather than tourists. The extended holiday was a test-run for them, to see if they could adapt to life in Venice. And it was a resounding success from that point of view.

Dan brought his laptop with him and had broadband installed in the apartment, thus enabling him to work quietly away on those strategic matters whenever he and Alma were not out exploring Venice's nooks and crannies. He also received regular phone calls from Neville to keep him abreast of the good progress that was being made on the potential sale of MSUK to Cresta plc. So he wasn't surprised on his return to learn that Neville had received a formal offer from Cresta. What did surprise him – and Neville and Jack – was the size of the offer. Three consecutive years of consistently high profits, together with a solid fund of reserves, had persuaded David Green that MSUK was worth six million pounds. Six million pounds! Dan's shareholding would entitle him to eleven per cent of that figure, almost two-thirds of a million, an incredible sum to retire on. It was a dream come true for him. And he had worked so hard for it. But for Dan McKay, life was never that simple. Nor was it ever that kind. There was a sting in the tail – a whole mess of stings, in fact.

To begin with, the offer was subject to the outcome of a process called due diligence, in which an army of lawyers and accountants hired by Cresta would undertake a thorough investigation of MSUK's assets and books to ensure that the company actually was what it purported to be. That qualification didn't worry Dan too much, but the next one did.

Only half of the six million would be paid upfront on the date of the sale. The remaining half would not be payable until the end of the next two trading years and only then if the company's accumulated profits over the two years matched or exceeded a level set by Cresta. If the profits fell below that level, the payment would be reduced proportionately. If there were no profits at all in the two-year period, there would be no further payment.

Then there was the method of payment. Only half of any payments due would be settled in cash. The other half would come in the form of shares in Cresta plc, and those shares could only be sold on the stock market with Cresta's prior permission, through stockbrokers appointed by Cresta and after at least a year had elapsed.

The terms of the offer confirmed to Dan that David Green was a very shrewd operator. The amount of hard cash Cresta would have to find was kept to a minimum, the shares issued to the sellers would be kept under tight control and there would be a built-in safeguard in case MSUK turned out to be less profitable than its recent track record indicated. And if the latter safeguard had to be employed, Cresta potentially could end up purchasing the company at the bargain price of three million pounds.

That last scenario was the real danger as far as Dan was concerned. His share of the sale halved to one-third of a million, only half of which would be in cash. If the worst did come to the worst, however, one-third of a million was still a substantial sum to retire on, wasn't it? Even better than Jimbo's pay-off for his twenty per cent shareholding. As for the shares from Cresta, he could hold on to them for a good while, see what happened. Stock market shares went up in value, didn't they? And when the two years were up, anything over and above the initial payment – well, that would be a bonus, wouldn't it? But after hearing the next piece of news from Neville, Dan saw any prospective bonus simply melt away.

Jack had declared that he didn't want to leave the company when it was sold. After discussions with David Green, it was agreed he could stay on indefinitely as Managing Director. And Neville could remain as Chairman for a temporary period. *The pair of them must really have turned on the bullshit to get the man to agree to that,* thought Dan. *He couldn't have chosen a more incompetent duo to take the business forward. Perhaps he's not so shrewd, after all.*

Much worse news was to follow, news that would put even a half-price sale in jeopardy. A number of executives, Vicky and Geoff included, phoned Dan in confidence to warn him of a worsening financial situation. New project wins across the teams had virtually dried up in recent months. Turnover was falling fast. Blaming the downturn on the so-called Credit Crunch, Jack had ordered all the teams to reduce their prices immediately.

The financial crisis that had erupted in America the previous year had found its way across the Atlantic and was currently dominating the news in Britain. But the way Dan understood things, the crisis (or Credit Crunch, as the media had dubbed it) affected the willingness of banks to lend and the ability of both companies and individuals to obtain credit. In his view, it was highly unlikely that the budgets of organisations in the public sector, which now accounted for the large majority of MSUK's clients, were affected at all. It was much more likely that the downturn had resulted from a loss of motivation among the teams, that loss having resulted, in turn, from the withdrawal of turnover targets, coupled with Jack's authoritarian rule. Dan knew from those confidential phone calls to him that some executives were already looking for new jobs. He couldn't blame them; he would have done the same in their position. No, this was a classic case of the Grandmaster Bullshitter allotting blame to everyone and everything, rather than to himself. And what could be more convenient and more topical to place blame on than the vaguely defined phenomenon that was the Credit Crunch?

But far more concerning to Dan was the price decrease instructed by Jack. With alarm bells ringing, he put in an urgent call to Neville.

"Do you remember years back? That phrase Jimbo always used – chasing turnover to pay the staff?" he asked during the subsequent exasperating conversation with Neville. "Well, that's exactly what Jack will be doing. Achieving turnover for the sake of it. But not making any profit. And profit is what the company needs to make."

"Look, Dan, I hear what you're saying. But Jack's in charge. He knows what he's doing, giving the executives a good kick up the arse. Let him get on with it, while we concentrate on selling the company. We're so fuckin' close now, so we are."

"If we let him get on with it, Neville, you won't have a fuckin' company to sell."

Neville's trademark silent response had signified the end of that particular conversation. That was back at the beginning of November, some two months after Dan decided to relinquish control of the executive teams. The last set of quarterly financial accounts he had seen confirmed that at the end of September, halfway through the financial year, the company was doing very well, having already made a substantial profit in the six-month period. Since the next set of quarterly accounts, reflecting the position at the end of December, would not be available until some time in January or even February, he would have a long wait to find out what damage Jack's mismanagement was inflicting. Meanwhile, the due diligence process was drawing to a close, with nothing untoward having arisen so far. Meantime, too, a meeting between David Green and Neville to finalise the terms of Cresta's offer was looming.

Later in November, Dan came up with a plan for the running of MSUK once it had been sold. It was his last-ditch attempt to ensure that the company turned a profit during the next two years. It entailed both Vicky and Geoff reporting direct to Neville and joining him and Jack on the

Senior Management Team, two sensible voices to stave off the worst of Jack's excesses when it came to key decisions. He emailed details of the plan to Neville. He also met Vicky and Geoff secretly in his home, when he informed them of the imminent sale, swore them to secrecy, set out his plan for the revised management of the company and encouraged them to open a dialogue with Neville as soon as the sale was announced to the staff. But it was all to no avail. Neville didn't respond to his email. And not long after, Vicky and Geoff each reported that Neville had suddenly stopped communicating with them. Dan suspected that Neville had revealed the plan to Jack, who had probably advised him in no uncertain terms to stay away from the pair of upstarts.

By early December, Dan had never felt so worried, frustrated and helpless in all his life. And he knew that the accumulating stress was affecting his health. He suffered from high blood pressure, something he only discovered a couple of years earlier, almost by accident. The medical profession knew what factors aggravated high blood pressure, such as stress and smoking and too much salt, his doctor had explained at the time, but they still didn't know what caused it in the first place. It was more than likely hereditary, he added. Since then, Dan had been taking medication to control the problem. But one morning while shaving he suddenly felt exceptionally weak, turned grey, was violently sick and took to his bed for the rest of the day. Dan was a man who never fell ill, so he didn't need much encouragement from Alma to see the doctor. By the time he did, however, he was fine again. Having learned about the impending sale of the company, his doctor simply advised him to relax as best he could over the Christmas and New Year holiday; the source of his stress would soon be gone.

Now here he was in his study on a freezing night during the first week of February – and the stress was mounting again. That meeting between David Green and Neville was due to be held the next morning. As requested by David, Neville would bring along a report on MSUK's latest financial position. But the quarterly accounts were late again. Shelley had promised to email them to Neville at some point that day. Neville would then draft the report for David and run it past Jack and Dan before finalising it.

Waiting for Neville's draft to come through, Dan had been on tenterhooks from first thing in the morning. He was a smoker. Although he had cut down significantly since learning of his blood pressure problem, he had smoked a lot of cigarettes that day, frequently climbing the stairs from his study on the lower level of the flat to have a cigarette at the back door and then coming back down to check his inbox for the umpteenth time. When he returned from the last such trip, Neville's email was there. He opened the attachment. He had feared the worst and this really was the worst. It was catastrophic. Not only had the company recorded a substantial loss in the three months to the end of December, but Neville's report predicted little improvement in the months ahead. He had nothing positive to say, nothing about any measures the company was taking to pull back the situation. It was almost as if he was saying, "My company is in terminal decline, David. It's not worth buying."

Neville was a notoriously poor report writer. It wasn't for the first time that Dan had completely rewritten one of his drafts. He would need to do that again now, but he was running out of time, beginning to panic and feeling dizzy. Then he remembered Neville's covering email, which he read again. *Jack says he's happy with it.* Those words hit him like a sledgehammer. How could Jack be happy with it? Unless... unless Jack didn't want the sale to go ahead. Had that been his game all along? Keeping quiet when the subject was discussed, nodding at all the right times, pretending to go along with the plan, but secretly hoping it would never go that far. What was it Neville once told him Jack had said? *It's what gets me up in the morning.* Of course! His empire. He would lose control of his empire. And so... and so when the prospect of a sale became highly likely, he deliberately sabotages its chances of success. The reduction in prices? Perhaps not stupidity, after all. Could it really be the case? Was he really not interested in the money from the sale? And declaring at the last minute that he wanted to stay on as MD. Was that just a smokescreen? Or his fall-back strategy? To hang on to his empire, even though he would have to answer to a higher level in Cresta.

Dan realised too late. Too many questions. His brain bombarded by questions. Then the tremor came. It began at his feet, rushed up through his body and into his head.

"Oh, no!" he cried, sensing what was about to happen.

A fireball exploded in his head. Pain. Pain so excruciating and violent it propelled him out of his swivel chair and onto the floor. He crawled towards the open door of the study. But he could only reach as far as the narrow space between the end of his desk and the wall, where he remained wedged.

It felt like an eternity until Alma appeared at the door. She had heard him cry out and had hurried downstairs. He could hardly lift his head to look at her.

"I think I need some help, hen," he gasped.

Chapter Nineteen

London, 2008

Sipping their obligatory mugs of strong tea, Neville and Jack sat at a Formica-topped table in a nondescript café on a nondescript London street. They still had the best part of an hour to kill before their meeting that morning.

"It always amazes me," said Neville, nodding in the direction of the building directly across the street. "Cresta is such a big concern, a major player on the London Stock Exchange, yet its headquarters are a couple of wee rooms in a serviced office in the backend of nowhere."

Jack shrugged. "I suppose it keeps their overheads down. Plus they only seem to have a handful of direct employees. The rest of their staff are employed by the companies they've purchased. Must be thousands of them by now."

Ignoring Mister Know-it-all, Neville went on, "Aye, a poky wee office in the backend of nowhere. A bit like your idea of a London office, Jack. No wonder it doesn't do much business."

"Well, there's the Credit Cr–"

"The fuckin' Credit Crunch. That excuse isn't going to last much longer with the guys across the road. Not after we've signed today. It's wearing fuckin' thin with me, that's for sure."

"Like I've said before, Neville, all the folk on the MRS Board are saying the same. Business is down everywhere because of it. It's a global financial crisis."

"And do they all live up their own arses as well?"

Jack let the remark pass. He took another sip of his tea before he changed the subject.

"Are we really going to sign away the company today? Even after they halved their offer?"

"That's what we're here for, isn't it? Anyway, as you well know, they haven't halved the *offer*. There's still six million on the table. It's the initial payment that's been halved, down from fifty to twenty-five per cent. Of course we're going to sign."

Jack looked glum.

Neville continued. "When I spoke on the phone to Dan earlier this week and asked him what he thought about the revised offer, know what he said? He said, 'It is what it is, Neville.' *It is what it is*. He's a pragmatic guy, so he is. And when I've finished here today, I'll be flying up to Edinburgh to see him and Alma. They've invited me to dinner this evening. I'll get Dan to sign his formal letter of resignation when I'm there. And that will be that. All the paperwork done."

"Well, I suppose otherwise you would have been delivering his P45. You know that we couldn't have afforded him if we had carried on without selling."

"You are a ruthless cunt, Jack, aren't you?"

Jack gave a tight wee smile, as if he regarded the insult as a compliment.

"How is Dan anyway?" he asked lightly.

"Do you really give a fuck, Jack? For a guy who's just gone through a near-death experience, I think he's doing remarkably well. Very lucid. And, like I said, very pragmatic."

"I suppose it was the cigarettes that did it. Whenever he used to come into the office, he was always nipping outside for a fag. Mixing with the other reprobates out there."

"Fuck sake, Jack, you know fine well it wasn't because he smoked, though I'm sure that didn't help. No, it was all the stress the poor guy was having to go through. With this sale business. With your shenanigans, starving him of information, keeping him out in the cold. And the sad fuckin' thing is that I was complicit in all that.

"Well, that's all going to change, my friend, once we've signed on the dotted line today. Starting tomorrow, I'll be in charge, I'll be making the decisions. And you'll be answering to me. I'm fucked if I'm going to end up selling my company for a quarter of its worth."

Jack smiled nervously. "I could always resign," he said, his usual threat whenever Neville decided to grow some balls.

"And I could always invite Dan back as Managing Director."

Jack looked even glummer.

Chapter Twenty

Glasgow, 2010

All that Dan could remember of the train journey to Glasgow was that he sweated a lot and felt nauseous. He couldn't remember the taxi ride from Queen Street Station at all. Somehow he had gotten himself into the car park below MSUK's office. He hadn't been down there before, but the place seemed oddly familiar. He was leaning against a pillar, sweating again – and waiting. *Waiting for what?* he asked himself. Sight of Jack Lamb striding through the near-empty car park reminded him.

It was the middle of winter, but, unaccountably, Jack was wearing a white summer suit. And he was sporting that beard, the one he had shaved off years ago. He was carrying a cardboard box and heading towards his car, a green Rover 75 he had bought brand new just before the sale to Cresta. His was the only one left in the car park; everyone else had gone by now.

Sight of the cardboard box also reminded Dan that today was MSUK's final day. *That's why I'm here. Of course! The box will hold all Jack's personal belongings, no doubt including that tacky trophy from the enterprise agency, the one he had hanging on the wall beside his desk. Well, that's all history now, Jacko, isn't it? The company is no more. It has ceased to be. It's expired and gone to meet its maker. It is a late company. It's a stiff. Bereft of life, it rests in peace. It's rung down the curtain and joined the choir invisible. It is an ex-company.* Dan laughed to himself as he misquoted from the Monty Python sketch.

Jack used his remote to open the boot. Dan noticed he was whistling as he bent to place the box inside. *Whistling? Fuckin' whistling? I'll be changing his tune presently.*

Dan didn't know how he had moved so quickly, but by the time Jack closed the boot and turned round he was there in the man's face. And it was a face that was suddenly white with fright.

"Feeling pleased with yourself, are you, Jack? Having killed the company stone dead? Having put... how many people is it, Jack? Seventy? Eighty? Having put them all out on the street? Well done, you big fuckin' cunt. Well fuckin' done."

Jack didn't reply. He seemed to be frozen to the spot, his face ashen now.

"I've waited two years for this, Jack. Two long years. To see if you could actually do it. To see if you could make a go of it. But you didn't have it in you, Jack, did you? You're all mouth, aren't you? Were you in danger of ruining the last company you ran as well? Was that why they threw you out, eh?"

Jack's expression was no longer one of fright. There was terror in his eyes now. He had seen the gun.

Dan looked at the gun in his hand. *How the fuck did that get there?* He hadn't handled a real gun before. But this one felt so familiar, so comfortable. And he knew exactly what to do with it.

He raised the gun and pointed it at Jack's head. "Well, it's time for payback, Jack. Payback for failing and thus depriving me of any more money from the sale of the company. Payback for the sleekit measures you took to give the company – and yourself, of course – a head start under Cresta's ownership. Deducting the costs of the sale from our initial payments, costs that should rightfully have been charged to the new company. Retaining our rightful shares of the profit the company managed to make in its last year before the sale. Oh, fuck aye, pal, you've stolen a shitload of money from me. And it was all to no avail, wasn't it, you incompetent arsehole?

"But most of all, Jack, it's payback time for my stroke. Remember that, you cunt? It nearly killed me. I had to learn to walk again, to take a piss standing up, to tie my laces. Every fuckin' thing. And all down to you. But now it's your turn to die."

Dan saw the dark patch spreading across the groin and down one trouser-leg of Jack's white suit.

"That you pissin' yourself, Jack? Never mind, it'll soon be over. By the way, Neville told me what you said about giving me my P45. Well, this is yours. *Solid thinking*, eh, Jack?"

Then Dan pulled the trigger.

The noise of the explosion woke him up. He was lying there in the dark, drenched in perspiration again, the duvet cast aside again. He listened for Alma's breathing. She was sleeping soundly. He thanked God she wasn't a light sleeper.

He had had the same dream countless times. His dream of revenge on Jack Lamb. But this was the first time he had actually pulled the trigger. It had been so realistic. He could almost smell the man's fear. Perhaps it was out of his system now. Perhaps he could move on now.

Of course he wasn't going to kill Jack Lamb, although the bastard truly deserved it. He had narrowly escaped death. He had his life back. He certainly wasn't going to spend the rest of it in prison. He and Alma had already experienced two very painful years since the stroke. And they still faced more pain in the form of money problems. He wasn't going to add to that.

So, the money. Dan often referred ruefully to the catalogue of events as his "nae luck story", a story that even a writer of fiction couldn't have made up. It began with the initial cash payment from Cresta. It was only half the amount he had expected before the stroke, before Neville's disastrous report to David Green on the state of MSUK's finances. Then it was reduced overnight by some fifteen thousand pounds, his share of the costs of the sale, which David had said should be treated as expenditure against the new company, but which Jack, with Neville's connivance, decided otherwise. Dan couldn't appeal to David, because the man died suddenly. He still wasn't sure what caused his death. The traders on the London Stock Exchange didn't know either. They knew only that Cresta plc no longer had a Chairman, so they brought its share price down – and down and down. When it eventually levelled off, it was a quarter of its value before the death. And it didn't show any signs of recovering quickly. Then, to cap it all, Jack decreed, again with Neville's connivance, that no dividends would be paid to Directors out of the previous year's profits, thus depriving Dan of another ten thousand pounds. Aye, the fuckin' money; it disappeared fast.

But Dan was the eternal optimist. Logic told him that those left in charge of Cresta – the Chief Executive and the Director of Finance – wouldn't allow MSUK to fail. All Cresta's other acquisitions were successful businesses. Surely they would ensure that MSUK was successful as well. Surely they would take appropriate measures if the company wasn't performing, perhaps even firing Neville and Jack. So, while the prospect of a substantial final payment from Cresta was still alive, Dan persuaded Alma to return with him to Venice – for a longer stay this time, one that would prepare them for a permanent move should that payment materialise.

They lived as residents of Venice for more than six months. It was quite an experience for them, but not a completely happy one. It may have been because Dan was still suffering the psychological fallout from the stroke or because they realised there were far too many tourists, many more than when they first visited the island a decade before, or because they discovered that the Venetians were very rude people, or it may have been a combination of all those reasons, but they decided on their return home that Venice was not the place they wanted to retire to.

Back in Edinburgh, they waited for the outcome. And while they waited, Dan received regular unofficial updates from a few of his ex-colleagues, Vicky mainly. Jack was lording it among his peers, the MD's of Cresta's other companies, passing himself off as a market research expert, speaking at key committee meetings. Neville was never around. The first trading year was a disaster, ending with a major loss, which Jack put down to the financial crisis; to poor, beleaguered Gordon Brown; to whoever the fuck he could blame. The second trading year went the same way. Neville and Jack were found out at long last, but it was too late. The company was closed down. A few staff were kept on, merged into another Cresta company, but the remainder, including Neville and Jack, were out of a job.

While all this was going on, the money was running out for Dan and Alma. Neither of them worked any more, but they still had a sizeable mortgage to pay. To keep them going, they had to sell those Cresta shares, even at their deflated value. Now they were in the process of selling the house. And the day it went up for sale was when the latest chapter of Dan's "nae luck story" was written. That financial crisis which Jack had been so fond of quoting finally caught up with Edinburgh's housing market. Before even the first viewer had set foot in the place, the likely selling price of the property had dropped sharply.

Dan shivered and pulled the duvet back over. He had gone through the whole sorry story in his head once again. Now he needed to get back to sleep. It wasn't a complete disaster, he reminded himself. They would still be able to sell the house at a reasonable price. Then they would move out of Edinburgh to somewhere where the house prices were a lot lower. Alma had been talking about the Highlands. That would be nice. They would be able to live up there mortgage-free and still have money left over. He would soon be receiving a good pension from his twenty years at the SNHC. Alma was also due a works pension in a couple of years. On top of that, they had two endowment policies which would mature in a few years' time. Not to mention their state pensions when those came along. All in all, they would still be able to retire gracefully, just not in *La Serenissima*.

Things will look better tomorrow, he said to himself as he drifted back to sleep. They always did.

Epilogue

Afghanistan, 2011

When the military transport plane lurched yet again, Neville's stomach heaved up even closer to his mouth.

"Are you okay, sir?" asked the young Lance Corporal sitting opposite him, the one who had handed him the paper bag to be sick in when he saw that Major Brown's skin had turned green.

"I'm fine, thanks," Neville replied through clenched teeth, trying, but failing, to smile.

No, I'm not fuckin' okay! he screamed inwardly. *Scared fuckin' shitless is what I am. And on the verge of puking my guts up in front of all these men, like a fuckin' wuss. Why the Jesus fuck did I sign up for this in the first place?*

The plane was circling above the mountains, a few miles from its intended destination of Camp Bastion in Helmand Province. A group of Taliban had been spotted near the camp, and it was suspected they had a missile launcher with them. The plane was forbidden from landing until the threat had been eradicated and the all-clear given. Meantime, it would have to ride out the storm that had whipped up across the mountain tops.

Neville took a sip from his British Army-issue water bottle and forced himself to concentrate his thoughts on something else – anything, other than being in the middle of a warzone on a plane that might be blown up at any second or might crash into the side of a mountain. Inevitably, he returned to the topic that had been occupying his mind on and off for many months – his post-mortem of MSUK's demise. The company – *his* company – was long gone now. It had been worth six million, but he had ended up receiving less than a million for it – a measly eight hundred grand, in fact. Thank fuck he had kept Market Surveys Northern Ireland out of the deal. Now that a proper peace had broken out in the Province, that wee business was doing very well, so it was. MSNI was still his bolthole, his nest egg; that had always been the plan.

When all was said and done, maybe MSUK was jinxed from the start. There was Jimbo going off his head in the Sahara. And Dan and his stroke. Then the company going down the pan. All those jobs lost. All those people, many of whom he really cared for.

There again, maybe it was him who had introduced the jinx, bringing Jack Lamb on board. Jack was the common factor behind all the disasters. The Jonah. Jimbo warned him about Jack. Izzy warned him. And Dan warned him. But he was blind to it. Having seen what Jack had done to turn round the Glasgow operation, he was mesmerised by the man and had a great deal of faith in his abilities. By the time Cresta bought the company, however, that faith had worn thin, so thin that he stayed away from Jack, letting him get on with it, letting him strut about trying to impress the other Cresta Directors.

Staying away. Maybe that was a big mistake. Even if he had stayed and got stuck in, though, it probably wouldn't have made much difference to the eventual outcome. Besides... Besides, he had other priorities to attend to. There was his family. The twins. His two beautiful wee blonde-haired daughters. Real blonde hair, mind you, not fake like Izzy's. And of course there was the TA. Not only was his long service marked at a special ceremony in The Savoy of London, but he was also promoted to the rank of Major. Then came the crowning glory of his TA career. His request to do a stint in Afghanistan was accepted. Because he would be there in a training capacity, he thought it would be relatively safe, but right now he was having serious doubts about that...

Don't think about the plane, for fuck's sake! Get back to MSUK.

What's been happening since Cresta pulled the plug on it? What about the bold Jack? He understood that Jack had set himself up as a consultant, claiming to be some sort of market research guru. Back in amongst his business cronies in Glasgow, no doubt. The Glaswegian Mafia, he used to call them. That greasy accountant, McCash – he was one of them. Maybe that's what Jack had wanted all along – to be a big fish in a little pond. Mister Research in Glasgow, he once called himself. Ah well, it'll be interesting to see how long the consultancy lasts.

Then there's Dan. Dan, the man. Fuck, he's been through the mill, so he has. Him and Alma have moved out of Edinburgh, living somewhere in the north of Scotland now. And what about the party Dan threw soon after the sale? A big affair in that hotel at the end of George Street in Edinburgh. He was invited, but stupidly declined. He wished he had gone now. There was a buffet, champagne, a free bar, even a jazz band. They said the wee man was up there crooning with the band. Bouncing back in style, so he was. Geoff and Hamish and Vicky and the rest of the gang got together and commissioned a poet to write a poem for him, which the poet read out at the party. A beautiful poem, apparently. Who the fuck gets a poem written about them? Heroes, that's who. Good guys. No-one would ever do that for Jack. Nor him, he supposed.

Dan's bounced back, that's for sure. I'm told he's reinvented himself as a writer, an author, with books published and all that. I'll need to get hold of the books and find the time to read them. Maybe one of these days he'll write a book about MSUK. There's more than a book's worth of experiences there. But then again, he would have to write about Jimbo and Jack – and me, of course. The Three Musketeers. Fuck!

It may have been triggered by the sudden thought of all his misdemeanours being made public or by the equally sudden banking of the aircraft, but Major Brown now found himself vomiting noisily into the paper bag.

About the Author

Brendan Gisby was born in Edinburgh, Scotland, halfway through the 20th century, and was brought up just along the road in South Queensferry (the Ferry) in the shadow of the world-famous Forth Bridge. He is the author of several novels and biographies and a mountain of short stories. He is also the founder of McStorytellers (http://www.mcstorytellers.com), a website which showcases the work of Scottish-connected short story writers.

Printed in Great Britain
by Amazon